To Mary Ann,
Enjoy a fast trip around the world in your mind.
Sandy Gelston

Hear You Think

Alexander Gelston

© 2017 Alexander Gelston

ISBN: 978-0-9996774-1-4

Major Characters Reference Guide

Reece Stanton - Protagonist; team leader; worked with Professor Quinn to develop the hearing device

Victoria Cannelli - Reece Stanton's fiancée; called Tori

Giuseppe Cannelli - Victoria Cannelli's father

Elizabeth Cannelli - Victoria Cannelli's mother

Professor Gabriel Quinn - Professor who developed the hearing device with Reece Stanton

Anne Quinn - Professor Quinn's wife

Henry Swenson – Reece's old friend, worked with Reece in the invisible ops, now part of the recovery team along with Greg Mays, Jeffery Harrison, and Sarah Castle

Greg Mays – Reece's old friend, worked with Reece in the invisible ops, now part of the recovery team along with Henry Swenson, Jeffery Harrison, and Sarah Castle

Jeffery Harrison – Reece's old friend, worked with Reece in the invisible ops, now part of the recovery team along with Greg Mays, Jeffery Harrison, and Sarah Castle

Bruce Hardy - Reece's old boss in the government, current boss of Reece's recovery teammates

Sarah Castle - CIA agent who is part of the recovery team; was part of the hearing device development

Frank Stone - FBI agent in charge of the explosion incident at Professor Quinn's lab

Jacob "Smitty" Smith - current FBI director

Dick Ycarte - former CIA director

Paul Sessions - current president of the United States

Ralph Winston - past president of the United States

Eyes Only Committee under President Winston for the Hearing Project:

- Ralph Winston - former president
- Dwight Temple - former chief of staff
- Dick Ycarte - former CIA director
- Peter Hughes - CIA agent (trusted by the director)
- Sarah Castle - CIA technical liaison
- Professor Quinn
- Reece Stanton

Emily Spring - current vice president of the United States

Roger Edwards - current chief of staff to the current president

Edward Trembly - aide to Roger Edwards

Sam Rodex - current CIA director

Harriet Venti - current Homeland Security director

Peter Hughes - CIA agent on the development of the hearing device; found dead

Charlie Wheeler - past vice president of the
   United States
Dwight Temple - former chief of staff to
   former president of the United States
Oliver Ellis - billionaire businessman, known
   as Diamond Ellis
James Wang - one of three perpetrators,
   manservant to Oliver Ellis, was part of the
   Ministry of State Security (MSS) in China
Fred Tsim - one of three perpetrators, was part
   of the Ministry of State Security (MSS) in
   China
Peter Huang - one of three perpetrators, was
   part of the Ministry of State Security
   (MSS) in China
Harry Yeh - boss to James Wang, Fred Tsim,
   and Peter Huang, the three perpetrators
   who stole the hearing devices; also was
   part of the Ministry of State Security
   (MSS) in China

Slim Williams - trash truck driver who serviced Aberdeen Proving Grounds

Jim Watts - Delta Airlines pilot

Natalie Matins - purser on Delta Airlines flights to Asia

John Collie - Air Marshal on Delta Airlines flight to Asia

Major General Jason Binder – 2-star general in charge of new weapons development at Aberdeen Proving Grounds

Colonel Eric Black - second in command at McGuire Air Force Base; reports to Major General Jason Binder at the Pentagon

Lieutenant General Brian Rest - 3-star general, Jason Binder's immediate supervisor

General Daniel Broadtail - Chairman of the Joint Chiefs of Staff (CJCS) at the Pentagon

Lieutenant General Steven "Buzz" Jeer - 3-
 star general, commander at Elmendorf Air
 Force Base in Alaska
Matthew Webb - Oliver Ellis' pilot
Christopher Cell - Oliver Ellis' copilot
Lisa Carter - Oliver Ellis' flight attendant on
 his G5 plane
Bolin Zhào - attending physician in Taipei
Michelle Dent - Taiwan US Embassy official

CHAPTER ONE
Prologue
Early Spring

Washington, DC . . . the only place in the world that has an alternate reality. It was one of those celebratory "in crowd" parties for the new administration. The spring was in full swing and the new guys on the block just couldn't believe they were now in charge. The giddiness had not worn off yet. With this crowd, it may never. It was not about doing the job, it was about having the job.

The new president and his administration could not possibly have been any more different from the recently departed administration. The noise was deafening, the alcohol was free-flowing—and the conversations were unguarded. It was just what the hosts wanted.

The Chinese embassy did not usually entertain. However, since they are significant holders of United States government debt and will be for years to come, the party by the Chinese government demanded that the A-list people attend. There had been a lot of "command" actions lately. The weapons sales to Taiwan by the last administration created an even more difficult relationship.

There may be a war being waged by terrorists, but the new administration was treating the main players like a bunch of disconnected criminals. It was a legal issue, quite similar to the Clinton approach to terrorism after the World Trade Center bombing of 1993. The first attack on the World Trade Center was prosecuted in criminal court. The guilty are in jail serving time. The 2001 World Trade Center attack was a paradigm shift in thinking.

The new chief of staff, Roger Edwards, was in the corner talking to Ed Trembly. "You would not believe one of the most hair-brained projects the Winston administration put in place."

"What is it?" asked Ed.

"It was classified as 'eyes only' for the president and limited to seven people. Normally this is so secret it can only be discussed in a SCIF. But it is so far out, it makes *Star Wars* sound real," said Edwards.

"What is a SCIF?"

"It is a room that is constructed as a Faraday cage. SCIF stands for Sensitive Compartmented Information Facility."

"Perhaps you should not discuss it."

"Waiter, I'll have another scotch. You have to admit, Ed, the waitstaff here is ever present and so responsive."

"Yeah, probably just military personnel in tuxes."

"Yeah, right," Roger scoffed in disbelief. "Well, I will just give you a clue then. It is a mind blower . . . like, what are you thinking?"

"What? You can't quit there!"

"OK, remember when we had a close call with the shoe bomber and we started having everyone take off their shoes, then the guys with liquids brought down six planes? Someone had the great idea to detect the perpetrators rather than the bomb. Then the underwear bomber created the brilliant new idea to view everyone using millimeter backscatter technology. We are back to the object—be it a bomb, knife, or gun—not the perpetrator. Before they could change course again, the administration's CIA had an idea and got a professor from a small, upstate New York college to work on a way to detect if someone was guilty."

"You mean, they would watch their facial responses to questions?"

"No, more weird and bizarre than that. Read their mind! The professor is to deliver it this fall. I can't wait to see if it works. I know it can't."

"What are you going to do then?"

"Unfortunately, nothing obvious. We can leak that the previous administration was wasting the taxpayers' money by funding absolutely stupid projects. It raises our credibility if we discredit them."

"Like the nuclear battery?"

"No, actually that is working."

"Oh, *Star Wars*. Shooting missiles with space-based laser weapons."

CHAPTER TWO

Saturday - Life is not what it seems

Just Outside Boston

"Oh, what a beautiful, fall day in Boston. I may love Schenectady, but I have so many fond memories growing up in the Boston suburbs," observed Tori.

"Nice weather, great seafood, lousy traffic," said Reece.

"Hmmm . . . what is bothering me? It can't be the visit to my future in-laws. Tori is the woman every man wants, a soul mate. This is meant to be, so it has to be something else," thought Reece.

"Reece, you are too quiet. What are you thinking that is occupying that mind of yours?"

"I'm sorry, Tori. It's nothing."

"I know you far too well. Fess up."

"OK, this is going to sound strange. I just was having a premonition of impending danger."

"You're right, it is strange. Sure, the former secret ops guy is now afraid to ask my dad for my hand in marriage. Honey, if I love you, he will love you. As for my mother, she is delighted that her doctor daughter is now on the marital path she has always wanted. With no grandchildren yet, she is getting nervous that she will only play with her friend's grandchildren," Tori said.

Reece replied, "No, I'm sure it's not that. I'll just take my mind off it and get back to enjoying this beautiful day."

"I know Tori will not believe that, but how can I tell her something I don't even know?" thought Reece.

The drive to Boston was uneventful for Victoria Cannelli and her soon to be fiancé, Reece Stanton. They were headed to Reading, Massachusetts, to have Reece ask Dr. Cannelli for Victoria' hand in marriage. It was a beautiful fall day in New England. The leaves had changed into stunning colors, as only the northeastern United States can boast. It had been a rainy summer, which had made the trees full of the potential of bringing forth the reds, yellows, and oranges that one can only appreciate in person. It was crisp, with temperatures down to the 40s at night and low 60s when the sun came out. It was the perfect time to wear a sweater.

"Yeah, Tori is right. My old life was so sensitive and covert that black ops groups assignments would have looked like rainbow colors compared to our assignments. We had ghost assignments. No color, no recognition, just satisfaction we were protecting the safety of the people of the United States. I sure am glad that is now past for me. I had a license to kill, which meant someone else had a license to kill me. I now have a great job at my alma mater in Schenectady, I have found a wonderful woman who wants to spend the rest

of her life with me. Things could not be better. Soon a house . . . and little ones to fill that house, to make it a home. Things are looking very good. Just relax, ol' boy.

The project with Professor Quinn is about as challenging as it gets. It's secretive, and that is one of the reasons he was so eager to have me work on the design of the ultimate weapon. I not only had the technical talent he wanted but the security clearance this project required. Knowing the president of the United States didn't hurt, either. That gave me the 'president's eyes only' clearance," thought Reece.

This was the day that Reece was awaiting with such anxiety that he had never felt in the years of working for the government. His last role was so sensitive that it reported directly to the POTUS. Reece was glad to be back into the light. Everything was "what you see is what you have." Well . . . except for the project with Professor Quinn. But that was his own little world with the professor, as far as Reece was concerned. No covert activity, no danger, just a great technical challenge. Time to be just like the rest of the people out there. No looking over your shoulder for someone intent on killing you. Get married, buy a house, have children, take vacations . . . isn't that what all this was about?

"The anxiety of meeting Tori's parents is not the total reason for my subconscious feelings. I have had that sixth sense all my life and it's saved me many a time. What is this foreboding? Well, we're almost at my future in-laws' house; time to get my head together. I do have to have my best first impression with Dr. and Mrs. Cannelli."

"Is this the turn?" asked Reece.

"Yes, then the fifth house on the right. You can barely see it from the road. The driveway pillars are usually the best way to tell people where to pull in."

As the young people drove into the circle in front of the large white house, Giuseppe and Elizabeth Cannelli heard the car coming up the winding driveway and quickly came down the steps of the front portico to greet them.

"Hello, my dear!" called Elizabeth Cannelli. She ran down the steps to great them. "I was so excited about your coming and to finally meet the man who has captured the butterfly. You must be special, Mr. Stanton; my Victoria has never settled for anything but the best."

"Hello, Mrs. Cannelli. Hello, Dr. Cannelli," Reece replied.

"Oh, call me Beth, Reece," said Victoria's mom.

Dr. Cannelli joined in with the familiarity. "Call me Giusep."

They entered the house, which to many would be called a mansion.

Schenectady, New York

If Norman Rockwell were still alive, he would paint a picture of this day. The ultimate fall day on a college campus. The leaves had changed color. The morning air was crisp. Today had a warm sun in the day to ease the pain of the eventual transition to winter. This weather had everyone thinking about more than academics… it was football season for supporting the team and having fun with friends.

The homecoming football game for a Division III team is personal. The players are friends with fellow students and professors in the stands. Yeah, Norman Rockwell could pick many subjects here. There was the young student manager of the home football team, making sure everything was in place so the team and coaches could do what they had to do—win a game. This was a picture of what college was all about. This place was everyone's mind's eye of what a college should be. So much so that a number of years ago, Hollywood invaded—or should it be said, *honored*—this campus with the filming of *The Way We Were*, starring Barbara Streisand and Robert Redford. It was even Hollywood's mind's eye image of an American campus.

This homecoming was against the archrival team. The Engineers were sure hard to beat year after year. The home team was called the Dutchmen. Education started in 1795 for the Dutchman school, whereas their competitors had been founded in 1824, a long time to develop a friendly rivalry.

The coin was tossed, and the homecoming team was to receive the kickoff. As the garnet-and-white-clad modern-day gladiators took their positions awaiting the football, the flags atop the stadium stood out with the strong fall wind. Oh, what a marvelous day for the college community! The fresh smell of fall was in the air, and the boisterous crowd was cheering their respective team. Yet, there were ominous clouds brewing on the campus. These clouds were not readily visible or even on the minds of the crowd assembled for a rousing game of football.

The crowd yelled and stamped their feet while the ball was in the air. It was tradition to be loud and noisy until the team received the ball and was either stopped with a tackle or a touchdown. Touchdown was preferred.

The kick was good! The young ball carrier caught it on the five yard line and ran the ball to the twenty-five yard line. There were very few big, fast guys playing here in this game; it was Division III, not Division I. The players played just for the sport of football. These were student athletes in the real sense of the term. The Dutchmen did have a player drafted into the NFL many years ago, to play with the

Cincinnati Bengals. He did get a good education, too. That was the purpose of this school.

The special teams left the field and it was now a contest of 22 men, with the crowd fully involved. The sounds were only silenced when the snap was anticipated.

The Humanities Building on Campus

Though Professor Quinn was known to never miss a game, today had a pressing task for him. During this game, Professor Gabriel Quinn had to finish testing the new prototypes, and could not attend. He knew by the sound of the crowd his team was winning. The sound of the football cannon always alarmed the local police and of course, Homeland Security. However, it was a tradition, and even with today's hypersensitivity to explosions, it was not to be put aside. When the Dutchmen made a touchdown, the cannon fired.

The government team that had ordered the secret devices was visiting on Monday and he had to demonstrate them for the client. Gabe had worked out a test sequence that demonstrated that the devices did in fact work. It was quite simple. However, only Gabe and Reece had used the systems.

Reece was in Boston for the weekend. He would be back late Sunday night. He was meeting Victoria's parents for the first time. This relationship may be going somewhere!

Reece was a particular favorite of Gabe's. He'd had him as a student in the undergraduate program some ten years prior. It was nice having his mind around again.

The advent of nanotechnology had made these developments possible. It took the special mind combination of Reece and Gabe to make what seemed impossible, work. Most academia worked on the "publish or perish" concept. Those who did not write usually brought in research funds. That was the reality, even for a small college. With a student-to-faculty ratio of 12 to 1, this school had to produce the outside funding, too.

This project, though quite financially rewarding, was so secret that most in the federal government administration did not know anything about it. Aside from Gabe and Reece, only the president and four other people knew of this work. The fact that this most stunning technical development had been accomplished would have to remain without any announcement. It was a matter of national security. Gabe thought, *Oh, to shout out the joy of what we did!* Reece was quieter. He just liked doing what no one else could do, and took pride in the accomplishment.

As the crowd roared for what was surely another touchdown, the sound of an explosion overtook the campus. It was not the celebratory touchdown cannon sound, either.

It was near the engineering complex. It was down the hall from Gabe's office. The epicenter was his personal laboratory. However, Gabe was in the lab, hidden in the humanities building.

The smell of fire and panic mixed in the crisp fall afternoon. Though it had been several years since the World Trade Center terrorist attack, the country was still not comfortable with explosions. The thoughts of everyone immediately drifted toward the terrorist mind-set.

Same with the Schenectady police. They were there as a courtesy to assist in security and crowd control. Now it was a different matter. The deputy chief of police was an alumnus, and always came as a fan. Now he immediately turned his professional persona into gear.

The chief approached the nearest officer.

"Find all available officers who are at the game. Then get the crowd secured here. I do not want anyone leaving this area. We have no idea what happened, but let's not make it worse."

"Yes, sir."

The chief ran to the humanities building. There was a fire consuming the beautiful structure that was the legacy of the first college campus to use the services of an architect to lay out campus grounds.

The campus police were already in place when the chief arrived, with the sound of sirens destroying the comfortable fall football day.

The Lab

The explosion was enough that Professor Quinn had been knocked to the floor and banged his head. He was starting to gain his presence when the Asian stranger came over to him and hit directly at the base of his skull. That would end Professor Quinn's life and his stopping this lab invasion. The other two black-clothed accomplices gathered up the three prototypes on the bench and set more chemicals on fire so this secret lab would also be consumed. This would keep the police and others from finding any clues.

The explosion was a decoy to get Homeland Security involved in the hunt for terrorists. No one knew what Professor Quinn was making, but the invaders did. It was now time to leave as fast as they could. They took off their outer clothing, dropped it all into the trash bins, and walked away as if they were just another group of hardworking students.

This was an international school, with many different nationalities on campus. Three Asian students was not an unusual sight. However, they had another way to leave with an incorrect impression.

Escape

The three previously black-dressed perpetrators quickly put on thawbs, flowing Arab robes, they had hidden near the entrance to the humanities building. These long, billowing robes would mask their identities. They also put on taqiyahs, Arab caps, they had brought, so they would appear to be part of the Middle Eastern students' community. Their caps were plain so as not to be noteworthy. As witnesses, most people would remember the clothing more clearly than the actual person. The ethnic imprint would be something other than what they were: Asian.

They walked away from the humanities building quickly, but at the same speed of

other people in the area trying to not be
consumed by what was happening in the
building they had just evacuated. In the crowd
they were not actually noticed. With focus,
they made it to the car parked behind the
memorial building in less than five minutes.
They now had to get off campus before it
became locked down. At this time there was
enough confusion that they had less than a
tenth of a mile to be on one of the city streets.
From there they had to go to the other cars
they had parked in the DoubleTree hotel just
south of the campus. From there they would
split up for each of their assigned tasks. One
was to implement the confirmation to the
client that the mission had been accomplished.
This confirmation was to be so noteworthy
that every newspaper and media outlet would
carry it as the headline for days. It would be a
blow to the American psyche of being safe in
the isolated American cocoon.

The other two were to venture to reap some financial benefits from having such devices. It was their bonus.

"That went just as planned," the driver of the car stated to his two companions. Both nodded their head in agreement. "Now, we must all be careful. We know someone will eventually realize what we have taken and will try to find us. Accomplish your tasks, reap the rewards . . . and see you in Taiwan soon."

They drove at a slow speed so as to be non-threatening. Police cars and fire trucks with sirens screaming flowed past them in the opposite direction without noticing them and entered the campus. It was as if a really big bomb had exploded. Actually, this was only the beginning of the havoc the American public would soon experience.

"I sure hope our client realizes what we obtained for him," said James Wang, the driver. The man in the front passenger seat, Fred Tsim, agreed with a smile. Peter Huang said from the back seat, "Now the fun really begins for us. We do make a great team. We must work together more often!"

Turning Stone Resort and Casino
Verona, New York

The Turning Stone Resort and Casino is run by the Oneida Indians on their reservation property. It was not subject to New York State or federal laws. It was, for all intents and purposes, outside the country. The casino is the most successful destination for gamblers from Canada, New York, Pennsylvania, the New England states, and as far as Ohio. No cameras, no inspectors, no federal interference.

Lately they had encouraged the big money people from New York City and from around the world to come to a very high stakes poker game. The minimum buy-in was one million dollars. The pot could be close to that, with some ten people playing. The casino underwrote the hotel, food, and drinks to bring these whales in to take their chances. The casino would get a piece of each pot as their compensation.

The casino, located in Verona, New York, is half the distance from Utica and Syracuse. The area is fairly flat, with the Finger Lakes to the west and the Adirondack Mountains to the north about two hours away.

Peter Huang finished his almost two-hour drive without incident. MapQuest indicated it would take one hour and 43 minutes to drive the 98 miles. Peter did not want to give the police a reason to pull him over. He stopped at the first rest area past Schenectady, the Patterson Plaza, to remove the thawb and taqiyah clothing. He had his slacks and turtleneck on underneath. He put the clothing in a small handbag, grabbed a burger at the McDonald's on the way out, and continued on his trip.

Peter stopped at the next stop, Iroquois Plaza, and deposited the handbag in the trash bin. He took time this time to use the men's room for the normal purpose.

As he arrived at the Turning Stone, he was greeted by valet parking. To support his image that he was a high roller, Peter used the service, and tipped the man with a $50 bill to make sure they knew he was money. He grabbed his seed money case with the one million dollars in cash as he got out of the car. It was a rental and did not make an impression, since it was assumed he flew from NYC to Syracuse. His Chinese ethnicity preceded him; everyone thinks rich Chinese come to America to play.

He walked in like he was wealthy, went to the reservation desk, and checked in. He, of course, got a large suite. The prices were low or courtesy for a high roller or someone from either NYC or Hong Kong. He checked in as being from Hong Kong. Everywhere else in the world they ask for your passport. Not in the USA. That would have been OK. He had one for returning home. Of course, it was not his real name on the passport he had.

Peter asked about the high stakes poker situation. He was told that he had to meet with the manager and get qualified.

"No problem. I'll be in my room," replied Peter in perfect English.

About 10 minutes later, the manager called Peter in his room.

"It would be good if you came to my room," stated Peter to the inquiry of having a qualification meeting.

When the manager came to the room, Peter had opened the bottle of single malt scotch from room service and was having a few sips.

"Please come in," welcomed Peter.

"Thank you. Welcome to Turning Stone. Since this is your first time as part of our Elite Poker Club, I have to evaluate your situation. I hope you don't mind," explained the manager.

Peter replied, "Not at all. I would not expect anything less. I'm assured that my fellow players are in this for the same excitement and have the equivalent resources to make it fully engaging."

"Yes, I can assure you they are of sufficient resources to be in the Elite Poker Club."

"I understand the minimum entry is one million dollars. Is that correct?" queried Peter.

"Yes, it is."

"Then be my guest in counting the sum I have in this briefcase." Peter opened his aluminum briefcase.

"Oh, a little irregular, sir! Normally members come with bank references and account numbers to establish their qualifications," the stunned manager reacted.

"Well, I wanted to play tonight and did not want a delay. I expect to have fun and do not want to wait. I flew in from Hong Kong. I was tired of Macau, and wanted to play against new players. Some of my friends told me about your club, with its different members. I hope this is not a problem," explained Peter.

"Not at all. May I take this to the cashier for counting?" asked the manager.

"Not a problem. How long will that take?"

"About 30 minutes. After that, I'll return with the equivalent chips and the access card to the Elite Poker Club. When you want to play, just call the front desk, give them your EPC number, and someone will come to escort you to the club. Since it's evening, do you want to have a courtesy dinner before you play?"

"Yes, that would be nice."

"After you have the EPC card, just present it at any dining facility and it will be our honor to provide those services as a courtesy," replied the manager.

In 30 minutes, the manager was back to Peter's room with the chips and the EPC card.

Peter went down to have a leisurely dinner at the TS Steakhouse in the tower. After dinner, he had the waiter contact the manager for the escort to the Elite Poker Club.

The manager was there within 10 minutes.

As Peter entered the club, it was obvious he was in the right place. He sat at a table with nine other players. He put about a one-quarter of his chips on the table. As the hands were dealt, he "listened" to each player either smile or frown. It was easy to learn the "tell" every player has when you know what they have been dealt. His strategy was to win some and lose some. However, over the long haul, he would be winning more than losing.

He played for about one hour and was up by some $300,000. This was still small change. The table had $10 million available, including his $1 million. As he was playing, he thought about how far to go. If he got greedy and cleaned the table, he would truly stand out. Also, he wanted to play again tomorrow. Better to take only $5 million to $7 million tonight. Tomorrow he would lose about $200,000, and on the third night clean the table. That would net about $15 million. Nice bonus.

It was fun to listen; *"Three kings, I'll take two cards for the full house. Four hearts, 25 percent chance of a flush. A great straight with king high going, just need the ten. Oh, skunked. Time to bluff this up."*

By midnight it was time to take the winnings—some $5 million—and go to bed. *"Fun, but not a standout. Some win, some lose,"* thought Peter as he excused himself and went to his room. He went to sleep with a smile on his face. It was a good day.

Albany Airport

Fred Tsim had his unit in his ear. It was a bit confusing to hear all those thoughts, but he thought he needed it to be aware if someone was following him. He was flying first to Atlanta and then on to Las Vegas. He was sure that going to a large hub, his trail would be lost. Atlanta is a major hub.

His checked bag had nothing to get anyone excited. The money he would use in Las Vegas was being shipped separately. It was the same approach that Peter was using. Cash does not have a history or leave a path. His staying at the Luxor would not raise any attention except when he started winning at the poker table.

The flights got him into Las Vegas in the late evening. He would crash the first night. Peter had the advantage of starting tonight. *"We all have the deadline to be out of the country before the event that confirms the theft happened. The team is certain that all flights and people leaving the USA will be subject to extra scrutiny. James projected that this was all going to happen on Thursday."*

That gave Fred only a couple days to make his bonus.

Fred gathered his checked bag and hailed a cab at McCarran International Airport.

"Luxor," Fred told the driver.

In about 15 minutes they were pulling up to the pyramid-shaped hotel. As Fred entered the massive foyer, there were people everywhere. The check-in area even had a line. *This city is like New York; it does not sleep,* thought Fred. He got a suite in the tower. This was important to create the image of super-big money. Just like Peter, his home was Hong Kong. Everyone thinks people from Hong Kong are wealthy.

He examined the suite. It had its own foyer, then a separate dining area with a bar.

Continuing further, he went into an open entertaining room, and further still he arrived in the bedroom with a king-sized bed. Then to the right he went into the bathroom with a tub and separate glass-walled shower. Almost every room had a large screen digital TV. He tipped the bellman and called room service. Sure enough, it was a 24-hour service.

"Please send up a bottle of your finest cab," he requested. "Yes, that will be fine. Include some cheese selections too," Fred replied when, given the name of their finest cabernet sauvignon.

When the wine and cheese arrived, he settled down to unwind. Tomorrow was showtime.

Short Hills, New Jersey

James Wang turned in the car to Hertz and drove back to the hotel he'd reserved for the night. He was not expected back at the house until Sunday. If he showed up early, it would give his employer reason to think that James did not go see the fall colors.

He had been Oliver's manservant for the past five years. His assignment was to get into the financial world in the US as a sleeper for a future assignment. It was now his time. His reward was the bonus he would get as his assignment unfolded. Mr. Ellis was a billionaire who did international ventures. He couldn't fool Mr. Ellis, so his staying at a nearby hotel was to permit him to keep his cover.

Once in the room, he felt safe. He called for room service. He did not want to go to a restaurant and chance being recognized. Perhaps he should have picked another location to wait out the night. He had not tried the new device yet.

He had to get to Washington this week and set up the "success" signal. He was quite excited that he would create such turmoil for the people of the United States. They seemed to believe they were invulnerable. This would prove to the world that they are not. He called his contact in Washington and made sure they were ready for a Monday operation.

Schenectady

Reece and Tori were in the car for the ride home that would last some three and a half hours. Travel is usually bad on the Mass Pike, but it was Saturday. Sunday it would have been a different story. Reece was more quiet than usual.

"How am I going to do this by myself? I can't. I have to contact Bruce Hardy to see if I can borrow the team. Then I have to contact Ralph Winston. Ralph, as the past US president, can open doors and help make things happen. How can I violate my solemn word to not share classified information? This is not going to be simple. I don't even have a secure telephone. It's going to be difficult explaining to Bruce why I need his guys right away, without explaining why, and doing it on a normal landline. The NSA doesn't even know about this project. I cannot let this get out to them in this process," thought Reece.

"Reece, how are you going to help Professor Quinn?" asked Tori.

"I cannot help Professor Quinn because I'm not a doctor," quipped Reece.

"Funny. That's not what I meant and you know it," replied Tori.

"OK, that's why I'm so quiet. I have to find a way to discuss a very classified project on landlines and get hold of some people to help me," Reece answered the actual question.

"So . . . the answer is?"

"My thinking is to first get former President Ralph Winston in the loop. He obviously knows about the project and I can discuss it with him cryptically so he knows the situation. I'm sure he still has a secure telephone, and he can then get someone to send one to me, and I can start with that," answered Reece.

"How about your old group?" asked Tori.

"The problem is they are not cleared for this project; and neither is their boss, Bruce Hardy," answered Reece.

"Is it time to break a few rules?" asked Tori.

"That's the conclusion I'm coming to," replied Reece.

"Can we save time and call President Winston while in the car?"

"That's one of the things I love about you. You're not only beautiful, but you come up with brilliant thoughts. Good idea," answered Reece.

Reece then had Tori find Ralph Winston's phone number in his cell phone. She hit the call button.

"Hello, Reece," was the always cheerful answer from Ralph Winston.

The two of them had lots of history. Ralph Winston treated Reece like a son. The relationship was always one of mutual respect and admiration.

"Hello, sir. Sorry to bother your morning in Idaho. I'm assuming you're home," answered Reece.

"Reece, you never bother me. What's on your mind?" stated former President of the United States Ralph Winston.

"Sir, this is going to be a rather convoluted conversation, since I'm on a personal cell phone and I need help on the Hearing Project. If you remember that program?" replied Reece.

"I most certainly do, and if I remember correctly, the delivery was to occur very soon," said President Winston.

"Yes, sir. The scheduled delivery was to be this coming Monday. However, it appears that the units may have been stolen, and Professor Quinn is in a coma as we speak," said Reece.

"Oh no! Sorry to hear about Professor Quinn."

"I'm traveling from Boston back to Schenectady. I'll know more when I get there," said Reece.

"What can I do then?" responded the former president.

"Sir, if the units have been taken, I have to find them and get them back. I need help. The only people I trust are the guys on my old team. However, they don't have the clearance that would enable me to talk with them. Also, I need to obtain a secure mobile phone so I can discuss this endeavor with other people, such as yourself," said Reece, clarifying the situation.

"Ok. On the phone issue, I can call the FBI office in Albany, New York, and have someone there give you a phone. I'm not officially in the chain of command, but I'm sure I can arrange such a handoff. Now, for your team; that does pose a more complicated situation. Though, I totally agree with you that those guys are precisely the team, with the appropriate skillset, to make the recovery possible. I have to think how we can do this. I'll call you back when I have done what I can," answered President Winston.

"Thank you, sir."

***

Idaho

Former President Ralph Winston thought about calling the current president, Paul Sessions, but that would be an affront to him. He decided to go around the new president at this stage. Obviously, Paul Sessions truly did not believe in the success of the project. Winston's approach would only involve the FBI. He called the FBI director, Jacob "Smitty" Smith. Smitty was still his man and could make things happen.

"Hello, Smitty. This is Ralph," said Ralph Winston in the most cheerful voice he could muster.

"Oh come on, Mr. Winston; caller ID has been around for years now. Great to hear from you! Do you need help with cattle rustlers in Idaho today?" said Smitty with a grin from ear to ear. Smitty was quite close to the former president. With a 10-year term that still had six more years to go, Smitty was still the FBI director under the new administration. FBI directors are rarely fired. The last one, James Comey, caused such turmoil that no president was going to do that again without strong evidence of treason.

"No, actually this is about a project that was classified POTUS eyes only," replied Ralph.

"Wow, serious stuff. How can I help? I don't remember such a project with you," said Smitty.

"My oversight. It truly was. As you know, as a former president, I cannot read you into it. So we have to work around that," said Ralph.

"Ok, someday hopefully Paul Sessions will read me in on this project," said Smitty with a tone of disbelief.

"Still believe in the tooth fairy, huh?" said Ralph, also recognizing that the current president could not put his ego aside for anything.

"The best place to start is telling who has been read in and how you can help him. Reece Stanton has been working on this project that yielded new high-tech devices. These devices were just stolen. Reece, as you know, worked directly for me with a team under the direction of Bruce Hardy. Reece needs two things. One, a secure phone, and two, his old team to work with him. Reece is currently in a car traveling from Boston to Schenectady. Can he stop in at the FBI office in Albany, New York, and pick up a secure phone? On the second request, this is more sensitive. Especially since Bruce Hardy is not read into this program either. Can you help me and contact Bruce to clear his team to help you-slash me in supporting Reece?" explained Ralph Winston.

"Wow. The phone is easy. I'll do that as soon as we hang up. Regarding Bruce, do I make it a request for FBI assistance or from former president Winston?" asked Smitty.

"Since the FBI is officially involved in the investigation, it can be an official request. However, when asking, use the subtitle of me with regard to a project I started that used Reece after he left the government. Bruce likes Reece, as do I, and will do anything to help him."

"I think that will work. For the record, Reece's name is sacred, even around here. His accomplishments, though many are not known, are extensive, and absolutely mind-boggling," said Smitty.

"Thanks, Smitty," said Ralph Winston gratefully.

"I'll keep you posted. Goodbye, sir," said Smitty.

Smitty did contact the Albany FBI office and told them Reece would be stopping in for a secure phone. The call to Bruce Hardy was a finesse.

"Hello, Bruce. This is Smitty at the FBI," said Smitty.

"Hello, Smitty. It's been some time since we've talked. How are you doing with this new administration?" asked Bruce, knowing it was the same for him.

"Certainly not as open and easy as with Mr. Winston," replied Smitty.

"I hear you loud and clear. Is there something I can do for you?" asked Bruce, agreeing.

"Yes, as a matter of fact. Our beloved former boss just called me with a rather unusual request. There was a POTUS eyes only project he had Reece Stanton working on after he left his position with you," said Smitty.

"I had heard Reece was working on something that included very leading-edge technology," said Bruce.

"Well, the devices that are the result of that project have been stolen. I was not read in on this project, as I you were not either," clarified Smitty. "However, the events around the theft do require the FBI to officially investigate. Mr. Winston has indicated that since Reece is the only one in the know here, he is the only one to actually pursue the perpetrators. To pull this all off, Reece has asked for his old team to be assigned to him to help out in this effort."

"So let my guys go work on something for a guy who no longer works for the government, on a project that neither you, meaning the FBI, nor I, can know anything about. Is that the picture?" Bruce summarized.

"Well said," answered Smitty. "Except it's sanctioned by our former boss."

"Who also no longer works for the government," added Bruce.

"Again, spot on," quipped Smitty.

"Sounds like my kind of a deal," answered Bruce with a smile. "I'll take care of it immediately, since it sounds like it's hot."

"Thanks, Bruce," said Smitty as he hung up.

Bruce immediately called the old Stanton team together.

"Ok, guys. You're going to get a call from Reece asking for help. I'm giving you clearance to do so. Just so you know, former president Winston called asking for this assistance. It's officially an FBI operation but we are supporting Reece because he is the only one around here read into a POTUS eyes only classified project," said Bruce.

"Work with Reece? Sure thing!" was the resounding response by the team.

***

Schenectady

Reece got a call from former president Winston telling him to go ahead and call Bruce Hardy. The old team was now available.

"Hello, Greg. This is Reece."

"Funny, Reece. I was just thinking of you," quipped Greg. "Let me guess what's on your mind. You need help from the team here."

"You're a mind reader," said Reece, trying to not let on the real situation. "I'm assuming we are on a secure phone network. Right?"

"Do you really think I want the NSA to know what I want on my pizza?" quipped Greg.

"OK, here's the deal, and I need help right now," Reece began.

Over the next 30 minutes, Greg and Reece discussed what Reece knew and what he did not know. They worked out the team assignments.

Schenectady

The team is starting to be gathered.

"Reece, this is Greg. I found the guys. The cameras on campus took me to their getaway car. The cameras in the area showed that they went to the DoubleTree, the old Holiday Inn, just south of the campus. They got into two other cars. One went on the Thruway heading west. That perpetrator got off at the Indian Castle rest stop and removed his Arab clothing. It appears he put it into a small duffle bag, according to the images of when he came out. Then at the next stop, which is the Iroquois rest stop, he deposited the duffle bag in the trash bin as you go into the building. Oh, how I love the 1984 world we live in that most people don't know exists!

"The Iroquois rest stop is about an hour away from you. Get there and retrieve the duffle bag. It's blue with red straps. There will be a thawb and a taqiyah in it. We can get

DNA samples off it for ID hopefully," Greg called all excited.

"What about the others?" asked Reece.

"A second one took a flight from Albany to Atlanta on Delta. The third is on the Thruway going toward New York City. Now get going before they empty that trash bin!"

"I'm on it. Bye." Reece signed off.

Reece was in the car in five minutes and on his way. He made it to the Iroquois rest stop within an hour. Not that he thought anyone would have emptied a trash bin on a Saturday evening. However, it was the extra contributions on top that concerned him.

As he pulled in, he saw two trash bins. He went to the one closer to the building and removed the top. Fortunately he knew from his previous dumpster diving it helped to put on latex gloves. He pulled his pair from his pocket and put them on his hands. He was lucky; the other bin must have taken the messy immediate dumping of people pulling in and emptying their cars of trash. There was the blue bag with red straps, just below a few items of paper that were not messy. No coffee cup drops. *"Thank God for small favors,"* thought Reece.

Reece retrieved it and took it to the car. While in the car, he put his plastic evidence gloves on and opened the bag. Sure enough, there was the thawb and taqiyah. He had to drive to the next exit at Little Falls to turn around and go home.

He got home and secured the bag in an evidence bag for later evaluation. He then consoled Tori and told her that his old Omega crew was coming to help. Henry Swenson was arriving at the Albany airport and he was heading out there to pick him up in about an hour.

Reece then called Greg.

"Any status on the person going south on the Thruway?" asked Reece.

"Yes, he just turned in his rental car at the Hertz in Short Hills, New Jersey. The address on the Hertz computer is—now get this—Oliver Ellis," said Greg.

"Wow, the billionaire?" exclaimed Reece.

"The one and only. Hmm . . . would he be behind this? He certainly would love one of these in a negotiation," asked Greg.

Oliver Ellis was known for tough negotiations and turning what was junk into treasure. He seemed uncanny in the global world of finance. He had the money, the skills, and the nerve.

"What did the person returning the car look like?" asked Reece.

"Ellis has a manservant. His name is James Wang. He has been with Oliver for over five years. It looks like him from the pictures I have in the newspapers on Ellis."

"OK, one goes west, another goes south, and the third is on an airplane to almost anywhere once he is in Atlanta. We are in a fix. I'm picking up Henry in a few minutes at the airport. Jeff gets here just before noon tomorrow, around the time you get in. We are going to have to split up tomorrow to follow these guys. The trouble with following them is they will know we are on their trail unless you have the antidote. I only have one of those. We'll figure that out tomorrow. I've got to go pick up Henry. Bye."

A few minutes after hanging up, Reece went to the airport and picked up Henry Swenson. The flight was on time. They returned to Reece's house. After Henry went to bed, Reece went to the alternate lab to do some work to help them in their pursuit.

Schenectady, New York

The Schenectady police escorted the team from Homeland Security to the college campus after they arrived at the Albany airport. Explosions usually mean terrorism. That's what the team from Washington was assuming. But a small college campus, an unoccupied humanities building? Frank Stone introduced the team to the chief.

"What do you want to do first?" asked the chief.

"Get to the scene," answered Frank.

As they came to the campus and the crime scene, they noticed it was now filled with the curious. If the yellow tape had not been in place, there would probably be people inside the building.

Frank and the team went into the building and found a devastated area where a small bomb had been placed. It appeared to be for effect and not for damage. Only the lab where it had been placed was like a war zone.

"Let's find out what type of bomb it was, and any tell-tale markings of who would do this. We'll work on motive later," Frank instructed the crew.

Over the weekend they worked diligently, bagging and tagging all types of material for later analysis at the lab in Quantico.

CHAPTER THREE
Sunday

Short Hills, New Jersey

Oliver Ellis was known as Diamond Ellis. He was a billionaire who would attempt to close deals with a bag of diamonds. The rumor is that the bag held about $100 million in diamonds in his house safe. Rumor also had it that he had ten such bags in his personal safe in his home office. Oliver was a long way from his hometown of London, but had done very well in corporate raids and acquisitions. He also knew that he was a target for his inventory. His safe was behind his large desk at the far end of his office. It was behind a beautiful painting by Behrens. It was *Surf Walk*. The subject was two women walking along the beach near the edge of the surf. Oliver loved art almost as much as making money. The money helped him with his love of art.

His safe required his hand on a biometric pad; he had a complex alpha-numeric sequence input that was 21 characters to open the safe. An online website indicated it would take 19 septillion years for a computer to crack his password. Additionally, to avoid his opening the safe when someone else was in the room, there were sensors in the area ifront of his desk covering to the entry door. If there was someone there, an alarm light next to the safe would illuminate and the safe could not be opened. There was a panic button next to the safe in the event someone tried to rush him from behind once it had been opened. The panic button released several non-lethal nets that were now the standard for police enforcement, as well as a series of cross shots of darts that temporarily immobilized the perpetrator. No one was going to surprise Oliver.

The only one permitted in his office was his trusted manservant, James Wang. James has been with him for five years. Oliver felt blessed the day he'd met and hired James. James arranged his life. Whether it was the menu the cooks prepared or the preparations for a trip on his G-V. James was also a pilot, and had supervised the modification of his G-V to go more than the 6,500 nautical mile range of the standard plane.

Oliver heard James arrive home from his visit with friends who had toured the fall foliage of New England.

"How was nature's show for you, James?" asked Oliver.

"It was spectacular! We saw reds, yellows, oranges . . ." James said enthusiastically.

"I just don't understand the thrill that has for you and your friends. A fine pinot noir, now there is something to behold." He smiled warmly. "James, I need to prepare for the next trip to Asia. Is the plane ready?"

"Yes, sir, I called before I left. They are planning on the trip on Friday."

Schenectady

The Arcanum Team is Formed

Both Jeff's and Greg's flights were on time. They piled in the car that Reece had, with Henry sitting shotgun. After the usual bantering, they pulled out of the airport complex and headed north on Route 151 to Route 7. When they got on Route 7 going west, they settled down and jumped on Reece.

"What's the deal now that you have us all here? Are you getting married this afternoon?" piped up Jeff first.

"I wish that was the case," started Reece. He continued, "As I said, I have been working on a project that was started by our beloved former president, Ralph Winston. It has a POTUS eyes only classification, with only seven people with clearance. They are Winston, Dwight Temple, Charlie Wheeler, Dick Ycarte, Agent Sarah Castle—she's a

CIA techie who advised Ycarte—Professor Gabriel, and myself."

Dwight Temple was former president Winston's chief of staff, Charlie Wheeler was the former vice president, and Dick Ycarte—pronounced "Cart T," with a silent Y in the front—was the former head of the CIA. The new president did not like Dick, so he had been replaced.

"That's a very close circle," observed Henry.

"Who in the new administration knows about the project?" chimed in Jeff.

"We don't know because the new president had told Mr. Winston that he was crazy to have even started such a pipe dream project. For all I know, only his cat and his mistress know—if he has one," retorted Reece.

The image of the new president, Sessions, with a mistress, created such laughter that they all calmed down.

"Ok, spill the beans. What are we chasing?" asked Jeff.

"I'm violating my security oath on this but it's necessary. I checked with Mr. Winston, and he will protect our butts on this. The Hearing Project was undertaken in response to the need to interrogate people to get real information. As you know, for the past few years, any type of interrogation has now been deemed torture. We cannot water board, deprive them of food or water; we cannot play loud music. We now have to provide prayer rugs, copies of the Qur'an, and guidance on the location of Mecca from where they are being held. So, President—I mean Mister, now—Winston, being the creative guy he is, contacted my old professor at my alma mater whom he'd read about doing new and different things with nanotechnology. When I came back to the area, Professor Quinn reached out to me. He recruited me, knowing about my relationship with Mr. Winston. The assignment was to develop a product that was so small it could fit within an ear. About the size of the Lyric hearing aid. The device would receive thoughts from a person," outlined Reece.

"I'm a first-class techie, but how do you do that?" asked Greg.

"The concept is quite simple, in fact. Nanotechnology made it possible. As you know, when someone is thinking, there are electrical pulses between the synapses of the brain cell connections. Those electrical signals are radiated like any electrical signal. The Hearing Project involved making a device that could detect those signals, amplify them, and feed them to an audio signal into the ear of the person wearing the device. If a person wears a hat with a wire mesh inside that's a Faraday cage, then the signals are stopped and cannot be detected. If you recall, the Faraday cage is like a metal screen that stops radiated signals. It's like the window on the microwave oven, in that the microwaves cannot escape the unit and leak into the room it's in. Therefore, with the hearing device, you're able to hear what someone is thinking," answered Reece.

"Oh, like wearing a tin foil hat so aliens can't read your mind?" Jeff laughed. They all snickered.

"The next question I'm sure you all have is . . . why? As I said, the government wanted to interrogate terrorist captives without torturing them but obtaining what they knew. If we ask the right questions, the person being interrogated will think about the answer, revealing the information desired. They don't know we are getting the information. We do this with enough captives, we get ahead of the game and protect the US from terrorism," continued Reece.

"The devices are very small. The challenge to us is to approach the person using the device and not let them know we're pursuing them. Remember, they can read your mind as you approach them. I have some techniques to help in the approach." Reece continued to describe his antidote and how they could use it to get to the targets. "We have to assume the perpetrators don't mind being lethal, and are therefore dangerous."

"How do you know who is thinking with the device?" Jeff asked.

"Just like when someone who's talking has a distinct frequency. Thinking also has a carrier frequency that discriminates one person from another. It's like when I talk, you know it's me. When Greg talks, his voice is different and we know it's him. Understand?" Reece answered.

Greg then interrupted the conversation. "I have the care package from Bruce. It's complete with our secure cell phones. I suspect President—Mister—Winston made the point of importance to Bruce to have such support."

"When we get to my place, we can assess the situation and come up with a plan of attack," stated Reece.

Schenectady

Reece gave Jeff and Henry capture kits. He had his own, with a slight difference. It had a number of items that were necessary to get close to the targets, subdue them, and obtain information from them if possible. Then they had to contain them for the proper authorities. They went through the details as if their lives depended upon it, because of course, their lives were at stake.

Greg, the ultimate computer geek, was to set up a command post. He was to return to Washington, DC, where he lived. He would coordinate everyone and all information.

The team discussed how they would now head out on the trail to intercept each perpetrator. The topic came up with what to do with the perps once they had been intercepted, and potential problems with local police. Reece did not have an answer yet but said he was working on that. First, get them, then figure out how to dispose of them. That's without killing them, if possible.

Reece was to head to New Jersey to determine what James Wang was doing with the device. Greg warned him that Wang was absolutely dangerous with his hands. Wang had been trained in the sanshou while in the military. He went further in his training into the more lethal variation of Jūnshì Sǎndǎ. This training made him a challenge in a hand-to-hand combat situation. Reece was trained and tough, but Jūnshì Sǎndǎ training made James beyond the normal encounter. Greg had found out that James was once part of the Ministry of State Security (MSS) of China. This is the equivalent of the Russian KGB. Greg would try to find out if the other perps were also Ministry of State Security (MSS) alumni.

The team considered that the perpetrators were testing the devices in such a way that could make a bonus for their efforts. Also, by them separating, it increased the chances of getting out of the country with at least one or two models. Greg found that person who was driving west on the Thruway exited and went to the Turning Stone Casino. That only confirmed their assumption of a test. If you could read someone's mind while playing poker, you could win every time.

Jeff was to head out to Turning Stone and get on the trail of the person who went there. They still didn't have a name for the person yet. Greg was working on that.

Henry Swenson would hop on a plane for Atlanta, trying to catch up with the person who headed that way. Greg would track that person through the airport and let Henry know where he was going.

***

Jeff arrived at the Turning Stone resort at about six o'clock. He was checking in, and inquired about what types of events were available for the night.

He had to find the target, but not reveal he was in search of him. He did not have the antidote. Reece had that. However, Reece did give him a device that would help him when he got close and could capture his target. Greg still did not have a name for his target; not that he expected his real name on the check-in at the hotel anyway. The DNA was on the taqiyah and thawb. The lab had not found the DNA in the database yet. *"OK, less than 24 hours is not unreasonable,"* thought Jeff. He did have a fairly good image of what he looked like from the camera captures at the rest stops yesterday. He had it memorized. He had to make sure he did not react if he saw him. *"If he has the hearing device in his ear, he will know that I'm targeting him. Hopefully Greg can use face recognition for determining the identity of the perpetrator. The Chinese have been using facial recognition for years to track everyone in the country,"* thought Jeff.

Trying not to bring attention to himself, Jeff innocently asked the concierge about a rumor he had heard about high stakes poker at the casino. When the concierge indicated that there was that available but it was by invitation only and subject to evaluation, Jeff laughed and said he would not be able to do that. It was just curiosity that had him. He then asked where they do that type of gambling. The concierge told him that it was off the normal gambling area, with an access card key. Jeff thanked him and told him that his wife's curiosity should now be satisfied.

He walked into the public gambling area to see if he could find a location that would be closer to where he needed to be. He needed to find the target as soon as he could. It was not certain if he would be staying here much longer. He'd arrived yesterday. If he wanted to win, he could have done it in one night. For all Jeff knew, he may have already left. Fortunately, Greg was watching the lobby area to make sure the target had not checked out.

Jeff called Greg.

"Do you know where he is now?" he asked.

"I can give you directions to outside the EPC room. He is in there playing now. There are cameras everywhere that I hacked into. However, they don't have any in the EPC room," answered Greg.

"That makes sense to me," responded Jeff.

Then Greg gave enough information for Jeff to find the entrance to the Elite Poker Club room.

***

Reece took Henry to the airport on his way south on the Thruway. Reece's destination was Short Hills, New Jersey. The question was, how was he going to capture James

Wang without getting killed in the process? It was important for all of them to stay in contact with Greg for his remote surveillance of each of the targets. It was not quite George Orwell's *1984* camera surveillance, but it sure was close.

Reece had a reservation at the Hilton near the Short Hills Mall. He would have to stake out the Ellis estate the next morning. Fortunately there was a store down the street with a camera; Greg would be on the stakeout, too.

Greg updated everyone that the airport perpetrator who flew to Atlanta was now on a flight to Las Vegas. That made perfect sense. Reece did wonder what James Wang was up to. There were the Atlantic City casinos, but he should have gone there first, not go back to his employer.

Henry was now on a flight to Las Vegas. Greg would let Henry know where he was staying once he tracked him. He now had a good image of the face and was tracking databases for facial recognition, as well as the target at the Turning Stone Casino.

On the drive down the Thruway, Reece called former president Winston to give him a status report and make a request for help.

Las Vegas

As usual, it was a sunny day in Las Vegas. Also as usual, there were people everywhere. Fred was now ready to play cards with his special helper. The team of three had agreed to not make any contact until they were out of the country. Fred assumed that Peter was richer with his bonus and would be leaving on Tuesday. Fred only had three nights to play. However, the stakes were higher in Las Vegas, so he could pull off the same amount of bonus very quickly. He did have the luxury to lose one night, like Peter. He had to lose and then win. Everyone assumes that the cards run in streaks, so a winning run and a losing run were quite normal.

He had check with the hotel to find out the details of large stakes poker games. Again, with Las Vegas, it was always new blood bringing in new money. His entry was similar to what Peter had done. His package with the cash had arrived and was waiting for him.

Henry Swenson was happy that he'd caught another flight to Las Vegas. Greg told him that his target, Fred, had checked into the hotel the day before. Henry was in the lobby working a slot machine without the dedication as everyone else around him. He watched Fred approach the concierge at the hotel.

"I'm here to play very high stakes poker. Can you help me find such a game?" Fred asked the concierge.

"Yes, sir, I can help you. However, we do have minimum requirements for those games."

"How much?" replied Fred.

"One million dollars."

Fred opened his aluminum case and showed the concierge its contents. "That turns out to be what I brought," said Fred.

"That's a little unusual, sir!" gasped the concierge.

"I'm an unusual kind of person. Please take it to the cashier for counting and qualification. How long will that take?" continued Fred.

"About 30 minutes, sir. Will you be in your room?"

"Yes. Please call when I can play."

"Someone will come to your room with the chips and take you to the game that's running tonight," said the concierge.

"Fine, see you later."

Henry was not close enough to hear the conversation but it appeared that Fred had presented the opening act to get into the card game.

It was up to Greg watching the cameras to tell Henry where and what Fred was doing.

Fred returned to his room. *"Time to put this device in my ear. When I had it in the ear at the airport I found all the conversations too distracting. I'm sure during a game, with perhaps ten people, the thoughts will be more controllable.*

I think I'll run the table at first, which should be about $10 million, including my money. Then lose about $2 million before leaving. If I leave after a losing streak, then the winning streak will not be as noticeable," thought Fred.

Promptly 30 minutes later there was one of the people from the concierge desk at the door to take Fred to the game.

As Fred entered, he thought he did not stand out in this group. It was an international game. There were two other Asian players; one from Hong Kong, and the other from Shanghai. There were two from Germany, another from France, a couple Americans, one from Brazil, and one from Japan. It was just what he wanted.

"Opening bids are without limit at this table," said one of the fellow Asians in welcoming Fred.

"Xièxie," responded Fred, thanking him in Mandarin Chinese.

They all introduced themselves and proceeded to play.

"Nice to have two pair with aces and tens. I have a Woolworth. I can't bluff this one." The thoughts were flowing. "I fold," said one of the players. *"Sitting pretty with a straight, jacks high. Not getting the cards that work. The new guy is getting my cards."* The thoughts kept streaming into Fred's ear.

After playing for six hours, Fred was up eight million. He won, he lost, but the steady wins made it a good night. At 1:00 a.m., they called it a night. Promises were made to come back the next night to even it out.

Henry had gone to bed at 10:00 p.m., sure that Fred was not going anywhere for the next day or two. Jeff called Reece and told him his target was still at it. They both must be doing the same thing.

Reece had the odd one that he was watching. No gambling destination. Why? The target returned home after spending a night at a hotel nearby. Perhaps his cover to his boss was to spend the weekend somewhere.

CHAPTER FOUR

Monday

The Campus

At 9:00 a.m., a pretty young blonde, blue-eyed lady came to the police scene, asking for entrance. She flashed her CIA credentials to the officers guarding the area. They were more interested in her than her badge and ID. They were not the first ones Agent Castle had ever charmed.

"Ma'am, you have to wait for me to get permission for you."

"What happened here?" asked Sarah.

"I'm not authorized to tell you anything, ma'am. Let me get the FBI agent in charge here," replied the officer.

He spoke into his shoulder mic and asked for Frank Stone to come or answer.

A minute later, Frank was at the entrance with a now very upset Sarah Castle.

Frank asked, "Who are you, and why are you trying to gain access to an investigation scene?"

Sarah showed her credentials and identified that she had a meeting with someone in this building at 9:00 a.m.

"Agent Castle, this is not CIA jurisdiction. As far as I know, Schenectady is still within the USA," said Frank.

"Ha, funny, Agent Stone. I'm here on an operational assignment, not to do an investigation."

"Who are you here to see? Maybe they can meet you somewhere else."

"Hmm. That's classified."

"Well make it unclassified for me or I cannot help you or permit you access to this building."

"Sir, you know I cannot do that. OK, I was here to see Dr. Gabriel Quinn."

"Well, Agent Castle, that's going to be a problem for you that's now outside this building. So coming in is not going to help. Dr. Quinn is in a hospital in an induced coma to help him recover. Say, weren't you once the rising star at the FBI?" asked Frank.

"Yes, I'm not sure I was a rising star, but I was at the FBI."

"It was the senator's daughter's rescue, wasn't it?"

"Yes, that was me."

"In that case, please let me be more polite. I'm SSA Frank Stone. I'm investigating an explosion in Dr. Quinn's lab. The first strange thing is why have an advanced engineering lab in a humanities building."

"I can help you with that, Agent Stone. He was working on a project for us. The working models were to be delivered today. It was so secret it was best to place the lab where no one would suspect a development lab to be."

"What were they?"

"You just came to the mother of all brick walls."

"How so?" asked Frank.

"Ever hear POTUS eyes only classification?"

"Only as a rumor. It really does exist?"

"Yes, as your rumor told you, ONLY the POTUS can waive access to the information that it covers. So, unless you have President Sessions' private cell number on speed dial in your not-so smart phone, I cannot go into much more with you."

"And though this is not classified, it's an ongoing investigation."

"Other than your word, can you give me anything that will permit me to share my investigation with you?"

"How about I call Dick Ycarte and ask him to call the new CIA director, Rodex, to then call Smitty—oops, Director Smith—and have your boss call you?"

"If you can do that, it will work."

Without batting an eye, Sarah had former CIA Director Dick Ycarte on the phone. She explained that there appeared to be a problem in obtaining the deliverables and that the FBI was investigating what appeared to be a covering explosion. She asked him to call the new CIA director or the FBI director to have the FBI director call the SSA on the scene to let her have access.

"I thought when they asked me to step down life would be easier, Sarah," complained Dick Ycarte. "OK, I'll call Director Rodex. He likes to be unavailable. I'm not sure he will take my call immediately. I'm not certain he was read into this project because of the new president's doubt of the success of this operation."

"Yes, I know. That's why I'm not calling him. He treats me like a dumb blonde. For such a sensitive administration, he sure is old school in his prejudices toward women, especially blondes, in that he thinks they are all dumb. Please, Dick, do this for me," pleaded Sarah. She knew Dick would move heaven and earth for her. Too bad the new administration gave him the boot and went with this classic bureaucrat. Sarah now announced over a few beers or wine, depending on the friends in attendance, that she now works for the CA, that's Central Administration, because there is no longer Intelligence at the top. It always gets a few laughs and nods.

Dick then called Sam Rodex's hotline number he had. The line had gone cold. He was unavailable at this time. So much for professional courtesy!

"Tell him it has to do with the Hearing Project," said Dick, pleading to the staffer, hoping that would make him respond sooner.

"I'll tell Director Rodex as soon as he is available," he replied.

Meanwhile, Frank Stone fell under Sarah's spell and her history. He took her inside and showed her the lab. It was a shambles. *"Nothing could have survived this mess. The devices are so small they couldn't have survived . . . "*

However, her instincts told her they were not here and they were out in the world. She thought, *"They are so small that all three could fit in your pocket without anything showing. Oh, we created a dangerous new capability. Can we put the genie back in the bottle? Whoever did this knew what they were doing. It was perfect. Take it, make it look like they got destroyed, and have the authorities chasing terrorist ghosts."*

Frank observed Sarah in deep thought. He really wanted to know what she was thinking. "I'm sure if I knew more, I could help. Some witnesses saw three Arab students leaving the area in a disciplined way. Walking without looking around, only to their parked car."

"Was this a red herring? Were they Arabs, were they students, were they the perpetrators? Only questions and no answers. The lab said it was a C-4 explosive. The detonator was classic terrorist design. Are we being played here? How do I get POTUS eyes only clearance to do my job? Perhaps Sarah can help without compromising her security clearance limitations?" thought Frank.

"Sarah, I have a case that I cannot solve without you. You cannot specifically tell me anything. What can you tell me that will help? Are there general information items that you can share?" Frank asked.

"Frank, yes, we both have the same assignment. Let's figure out a way, without the bureaucratic limitations. As I said, we are the lead agency in the development and as of today, the delivery, of three devices that are such leading-edge technology that it required the POTUS eyes only classification. I was to pick up those three devices today. My theory is that whoever created this mess was just covering up the theft, and tried to kill the thick-skulled Dr. Quinn as a bonus. He was hit on the head at the base of the skull. It was thick alright."

Frank looked at her intently, nodding his head to indicate she should go on.

"No, I cannot tell you what they stole. However, the size is that of an insertable hearing aid. On the market is a Lyric hearing aid that's so small it's in the ear, and not in any way noticeable. They are that size. So, if they are here, it will be almost impossible to find them without Dr. Quinn. The greater likelihood is that they are now missing," explained Sarah.

"Are they dangerous?" asked Frank.

"You mean as a weapon?" replied Sarah.

"Yes."

"No, but they are so unique, and have such implications for anyone who has them."

"That clears up a lot," joked Frank. "Now I know it's a needle, in or out of a haystack."

"Was there any evidence left behind, and do you have any information on the perpetrators?" asked Sarah.

"It was a very professional job. In and out, nothing left behind. Ghosts. What better way to leave than to fit into a college campus with students from all around the world? No one and everyone sticks out," sighed Frank.

***

About four hours later, Dick Ycarte received a call from the new CIA director, Sam Rodex.

"Dick what was the purpose of your call to me? I have never heard of the Hearing Project. Is this something you forgot to transfer to me?"

Dick was caught off guard. He had assumed the new president, Paul Sessions, had briefed him on this project. But he was right in his original intuition; the new president had not. With the classification as POTUS eyes only, Dick did not have the authority to reveal any details to his replacement, Sam Rodex. Only the new president did.

"Sam, it was something that I had in my mind and in the meantime, I realized the project had been shelved."

"Why did you then call on the hotline number?"

"Chalk it up to an old fool who should be retired. Sorry to have bothered you. I'll call on the regular line if I do need to talk to you again. However, thanks for calling me back."

After hanging up, Dick realized that Sarah was out there by herself. She had to know. Dick then called Sarah Castle.

"Sarah, I hate to break the news to you, but Director Rodex was not briefed on the Hearing Project by President Sessions. You're an agent without an organization. I'll talk to Ralph Winston about this and why Sessions did not bring Rodex into this project. I'm sure Sessions was briefed by our former boss, former president Winston, on this. I suspect that Rodex discounted the reality of being successful and just did not bring anyone onboard to its existence. Only a former president to the new president conversation is going to be effective," said Dick.

"Oh, wow! Talk about bungling at the top. As you know, only the current president can grant the POTUS eyes only clearance. Not even the ex-president can do that. That means I cannot even tell my boss," moaned Sarah.

"That's right. Did you ever use your direct report access to then-president Winston for this project?"

"Yes, but I only did it a couple times on the technical progress and the milestone schedule."

"That means that Mr. Winston has to help us. It would help us to have the current president, President Sessions, bring your boss into the fold on this project. I'll call the former president and explain this to him and ask for his help."

"Thanks, I'll just work as much as I can."

***

"Hello, Mr. Winston. This is Dick Ycarte," said Dick to former president Winston.

"Yes, I know who it is. My phone still has caller ID . . . and I do miss the sound of your voice," Ralph joked.

"Yes, sir, I'm sorry it's so early in Idaho."

"Oh, come on, Dick. You remember we cowboys get up early. This is not early for me. I'm already on my third cup of coffee. Now, why did you call me, other than to see how I am?"

"Sir, do you remember the Hearing Project?"

"Of course I do. I was so disappointed that it was not finalized under my watch. How is the program going?"

The former president always played his cards carefully. He had heard the latest from Reece, but did not want to expose his source of such classified information.

"Sir, I'm assuming your phone is still classified secure. Is that so?"

"Yes, they did not take that away from me. Probably because someone forgot to do that," Ralph laughed.

"OK, sir. The project was to have three deliverables given to Agent Sarah Castle today," explained Dick.

"I remember her. She helped rescue that senator's daughter. Everyone really remembers her once they have any contact with her. There's a young lady with a future," commented the former president.

"Yes, she is all of what you say. She arrived at the college today for the handoff. Unfortunately, the school experienced a bomb blast in the lab, and Dr. Quinn was injured," said Dick.

"Oh no, is he going to make it?" asked the former president with concern.

"Yes. He is in a coma, but looks like he will make it."

"What about the deliverables?"

"It's unknown at this time. It's Sarah's opinion that the units were stolen, and the bomb blast in the lab was to cover up the theft. The perpetrators hit Dr. Quinn, assuming it would kill him. Fortunately, it did not."

"From what you're telling me, I would agree with Sarah. I might add, I heard about this from Reece Stanton on Saturday. He is already assuming the same thing as Sarah is. Both are classified cleared for this project. So, how can a former president help you?" shared Ralph Winston. He realized that Dick was sharing information with him, and now he should do likewise.

"Well, sir, I called the new director of the CIA, Sam Rodex, about the theft today. I only used the term Hearing Project. He said he had not heard of such a project. As you know, I cannot tell him about it. Only the new president can, and for some reason, President Sessions did not tell the new CIA director."

"Ooh, that puts Sarah in a bind. She cannot even tell her boss, only President Sessions," said Winston.

"Exactly! What a screw-up by President Sessions."

"OK, I'll call him and try to fix this. Dick, as I said, the professor's assistant on this project is a name from our past. It's Reece Stanton. He is read into this project, and working on the retrieval of the devices. We should hook Sarah up with him. I also need the FBI to be aware of what we are doing," said former president Winston. "Thanks, Dick, good to hear from you. Call me more often; remember, I'm retired."

The former president placed a call for current President Sessions.

"White House, how may I direct your call?"

"Hello, this is Ralph Winston. I would like to talk with President Sessions."

"Yes, Mr. Winston, I'll put you through to his office."

"Hello, President Sessions' office. How may I help you?"

"Hello, this is Ralph Winston. Is President Sessions available?"

"Oh hello, Mr. Winston. Nice to hear your voice. I'm sorry, President Sessions is in a briefing meeting. Can I have him call you when it's over, in about 10 minutes?"

"That would be great. Have him make the call on a secure line to my secure cell phone. Thank you."

"Will do, sir."

Ten minutes later, President Sessions called former president Winston.

"Hello, Paul," Ralph Winston said, answering on his cell phone.

"Hello, Ralph. What is the crisis that makes you call so early from Idaho?"

"I'm sure it's an oversight, but you have a dilemma on your hands."

"What is it?" replied President Sessions.

"There was an ongoing project named Hearing Project that was being handled by the CIA. Do you recall that project?"

"Can't say I do."

"It had to do with the development of a device that permitted someone to read another person's mind. It was being developed at an upstate New York college by a genius professor. Do you remember that?"

"Oh, yes, I do. A real *Star Wars* idea and a reality stretch. I thought it was one of your harebrained projects going nowhere."

"Paul, it's not harebrained, and is a reality,"

"What do you mean?"

"It was completed."

"Well excuse my being skeptical. What is the problem?"

"Who have you briefed on this project?"

"Just my chief of staff, Roger Edwards."

"Not the replacement at the CIA, Sam Rodex?"

"Of course not! The CIA only has jurisdiction outside the USA. It does not belong in their bailiwick."

"I put it there because I trusted their ability to keep it under wraps and use it on international terrorists."

"I don't have the same confidence in those people."

"You have one CIA person, who was the technical liaison to me, who knows about it, and was to receive the deliverables today."

"Ok, and the problem is what?"

"There appears to have been a theft of the deliverables on Saturday, and no one in charge knows anything and what the real problem is at that college."

"Hmmm, why is that a crisis?"

"Paul, did you hear me? These devices mean any person can read another person's mind!"

"Are you sure they work, Ralph?"

"Paul, I know both Dr. Quinn and Agent Castle. She would not be there unless they are working."

"What do you want me to do?"

"First, bring Sam Rodex in on this so Agent Castle can talk to him. Then contact her and let her know you're there to help her. In case you don't recall, this project is classified as POTUS eyes only. You're the only one who can reveal this project or its details to anyone. Let Sarah know that Sam is now cleared. There is an FBI agent on the scene too who needs clearance. His name is Frank Stone. He is with Agent Castle."

They hung up, and President Sessions proceeded to call Sam Rodex to come to the Oval Office ASAP.

Then he called Agent Sarah Castle.

"Hello, Agent Castle," answered Sarah.

"This is the White House, please hold for the president," the White House operator told her.

"Hello, Agent Castle. This is President Sessions. I understand you have a project that you need help on. I'm also assuming you have a secure phone."

"Yes, sir, on both accounts. I'm here to pick up three deliverables for the Hearing Project."

"President Winston asked me to brief CIA Director Rodex on the Hearing Project. He is due here in the next 20 minutes. I'll do that. What else can I do?"

"I'm working with Frank Stone from the FBI. I need you to talk with him to let me work with him on the case here. It's your call if you want to brief him on the Hearing Project so we can fully collaborate on the case. We are already two days behind the perpetrators."

"I can clear the way for him to work fully with you. I'm not sure I'll clear him for the Hearing Project."

"Thank you, sir."

"Is Frank Stone nearby?" asked the president.

"Yes, about 50 feet away,"

"Let me talk with him, please."

Sarah shouted to Frank to come talk on her phone.

"Hello, this is Frank Stone," answered Frank.

"Hello, Agent Stone, this is President Sessions."

"What can I do for you, sir?"

"Agent Stone, I understand Agent Castle is there and she needs you to cooperate with her on your case."

"Yes, that's true."

"Please assist her in any way you can on your case."

"Yes, sir, I'll do that."

"Thank you, Agent Stone."

Sessions still showed his disbelief in the project by forgetting to read SSA Stone in on the project. This oversight was going to be a challenge for Sarah.

Frank hung up and turned to Sarah.

"OK, I only expected my boss to call, not the top dog. You've got friends in all the right places! Now let's work together," exclaimed Frank Stone.

"Frank, unfortunately, it's still a one-way relationship. The president did not give me clearance to share what I know. However, we can find a way to make this work."

Washington, DC

James Wang came out of the mansion at about 9:00 a.m. He headed east on Interstate 78 toward Newark airport. *"Maybe he is headed out of town,"* thought Reece. With so much traffic, it was easy to trail Wang without being discovered. After about seven minutes, Reece had his answer. Wang then turned onto Interstate 95 going south. He was headed to another location. After following about 45 minutes, he got his answer. Wang did not take the Interstate 295 exit, which was the way to go to Atlantic City. Wang instead stayed on I-95. His speed was at the traffic flow of 70 to 75. Reece had to do the same or lose him. Of course if he did, he was confident that Greg could find him again.

Greg updated everyone that the perpetrator at the Turning Stone was Peter Huang. The perpetrator now in Las Vegas was Fred Tsim. Greg thought, *"Thanks, China, for having such an affinity for controlling everyone. With their extensive facial recognition and database, it made it easy for me once I hacked their computers."*

All three perpetrators were formerly with the Chinese Ministry of State Security (MSS). All three were very resourceful and were considered dangerous. Like James Wang, they had skills in sanshou from their time in the military. Greg distributed files and pictures of all three to the field team. It was now certain that they were up against some professionals. With the hearing devices, the targets had the upper hand.

Reece stayed as close to Wang as he could when he got to Washington, DC. This was more difficult because there were traffic lights that could separate them easily. Reece gave Greg an update on where he was. Reece now had to depend on Greg's ability to hack into the DC traffic cameras.

When Wang got to DuPont Circle, he went into the DuPont Circle Hotel. That was a lot better than the subway system that had a stop at DuPont Circle. Reece's target was doing things differently than the other two targets. *"What is he up to?"* thought Reece. Reece asked Greg to see what he could see on the lobby cameras. Greg came back with a response that he was meeting with a short Asian man about 35 years old. He was wearing glasses as thick as Coke bottles. *"Oh boy, a real Mutt and Jeff combination,"* thought Reece, because Wang was very tall for most Chinese and this guy was comparatively shorter.

***

As James Wang drove from Short Hills to Washington, he called his contact to obtain the information on the Aberdeen Project. He was told they were in place and were executing the theft as outlined. They then met at the DuPont

Circle Hotel and talked for a few minutes. After about five minutes they came out and walked down Connecticut Avenue for a couple blocks to examine the target area. When they got to Lafayette Park, they looked around at the park and the surrounding area.

This was dangerous for Reece, but this was where he'd have to watch on foot. He followed them; it was not hard seeing Mutt and Jeff in the crowd. Reece was fairly certain that Wang did not have the device in his ear. However, he did put on his special baseball cap. Everyone wears baseball caps now, even indoors.

As he got into the entrance to Lafayette Park, he watched them walk around on the White House side. It was time for Reece to sit down on a bench and "read" a book.

"Is the driver set up?" James asked his short contact.

"As we speak, it's being arranged."

"Great, we ready for Project Retrieve?"

"The men are in place."

***

Baltimore

Slim Williams met with his drug dealer as usual, but this time he was confronted with a request that had to be followed. He was now told that some people would let his employer know about his drug habit if he did not cooperate. The name Slim was not a description of the physical nature of the person. He was actually about 275 pounds on a 5' 9" frame. The Slim was someone's joke many years ago when his gray hair was brown.

"Slim, I have some friends who want a ride in your truck when you go into the Aberdeen Proving Grounds."

"They can't get into the facility without the proper paperwork."

"They will not be in the seat with you. Arrangements have been made to modify your truck to have a small compartment in the trash section. They will ride in there."

"When is this to happen?" asked Slim.

"Tomorrow. They will meet you at the McDonald's on Philadelphia Boulevard at 7:00 a.m. Tuesday is your normal day for pickup, so nothing will be out of place."

"OK," agreed Slim, with no choice but to cooperate. He could not lose his job. He had a wife and three beautiful children. The middle one, his daughter, he worshipped. He was trying very hard for her sake to stop the drug habit. It was hard, but he was getting closer every day.

Hong Kong

Harry Yeh had stayed at the Harbour Grand Hotel on Oil Street many times. It was a five-star facility. The hotel was just off the harbor. The harbor view from many rooms was breathtaking. The lobby was not designed for meeting someone because there were no chairs or couches for sitting. It did provide a secure intersection of people without having someone waiting to observe the meeting. The Ministry of State Security employed Harry. He had put together a team to take advantage of the new capitalist environment in China. Why should only the manufacturers and others in his country make substantial income with the new capitalist rules? Their talents could satisfy a market.

Harry went up the stairs near the harp that was played many times, creating a cultured ambience. He had also been at the hotel when a piano was the music option. As he passed the harp, he saw his client approach. He turned around and went down the stairs to the hotel restaurant with his client.

The client asked, "Have you been successful?"

"Yes, we have. The units are being tested as we speak," replied Harry.

"What will you do that will prove that before we take delivery?" asked the client.

"This Thursday, every news outlet in the world will cover as the front page or lead item what we did to prove that we were successful," Harry said with confidence.

"What do you mean?"

"Let's just say that the government of the US will be shaken to its core." Harry answered with a cunning smile.

"What is the expected delivery date?" asked the client.

"This weekend," answered Harry.

Both client and Harry never smiled. However, upon hearing this news, both men came forth with a smile to show they were pleased that they were close to accomplishing the goal.

Harry returned to China, and the client went to his yacht in the harbor.

Washington, DC - The White House

President Sessions welcomed CIA Director Sam Rodex into the Oval Office.

"Sit down, Sam. Want a cup of coffee?" welcomed the president.

"Thank you, sir. Black please," replied Sam.

"Sam, I have a project that I was remiss in discussing with you during our initial briefing. It was a project that I had dismissed as not being a valid, successful project. It's named the Hearing Project."

"Dick Ycarte called me about that earlier today. He indicated that it was complete and not to worry."

"Well, he was right and wrong. The project was complete in that some new devices we contracted to have developed and manufactured were to be delivered today. The worry part is not accurate," replied the president.

He continued, "This project is classified as POTUS eyes only. In this administration, so far it's only you now and my chief of staff, Roger Edwards, who know. The past administration had Agent Sarah Castle, a techie at the CIA, and your predecessor, Dick Ycarte."

"I know of Agent Castle; I did not know what her assignment was, but she is well thought of in the hallways."

"She now realizes that you're cleared to the project. I'm sorry I left it off the list. I just did not think anyone could develop such a device successfully. It just made me think that you had enough on your plate."

"So what is the worry part about?"

"That's what brought this to my attention. Agent Castle went to the college to take possession of the three deliverable models. When she got there, she found out the development lab had been bombed, the developing professor was in a coma, and the models were nowhere to be found. They are presumed to have been taken by the people who planted the bomb and tried to kill Professor Quinn. We have to worry about who was behind this and where those first models are."

"Sure you're not offering scotch and not coffee, sir? That's major league worry," observed Sam.

"What is happening now is, the FBI is working on leads for this theft. The SSA is Frank Stone. Agent Castle is helping him. I have not cleared Frank on the Hearing Project. Agent Castle is involved in aiding the investigation without revealing the project's details. Let's hope they can do it. Unfortunately, we are two days behind the perpetrators," continued the president.

Turning Stone
Monday Evening

Peter Huang did lose $300,000 the night before. The fellow card players did not show sympathy, since he almost cleared the table on Saturday night. As the game proceeded, Peter was slowly but steadily winning everything tonight. At about 1:00 a.m., he had the pot up to $2 million. It was time to clear the table.

"The way the Asian is playing, I'm not sure my three kings will take him," thought the man from Manhattan. "I'll take two cards," he then said.

"I'll stand pat," the next man said. *"A flush with queen high would work in most games. However, the Asian seems to know our cards. I think I'll stay in and find out,"* thought the liquor wholesale man from New Jersey.

Peter thought, *"My full house, aces and jacks, are unbeatable. Time to finish this up and go to bed."*

"Call," was the statement around the table. Then Peter showed his full house. "Ah!" was the cry in unison.

"I think I'll call it a night while I'm ahead," stated Peter. Three men asked quickly, "Will you be back tomorrow night to give us a chance to even it up?"

"Of course I will. Just bring more money," replied Peter, knowing that by tomorrow early in the afternoon no one would know he'd left with about $15 million of their money.

Las Vegas

Henry observed his target doing the same thing Jeff had reported for his target. Get up casually, have a nice meal, go play poker, and go to bed. Reece, on the other hand, was following his target to Washington, DC. Henry did watch his target, Fred, at a distance. Reece did not tell him the device range, but with so many other people in the area and others much closer, he thought he was not being detected. It was like playing with fire. You will get burned if you get too close.

That night, Fred went to the high stakes poker game as he had the night before. Henry could tell by the comments coming out last night that Fred was a big winner. "*Oh, surprise,*" thought Henry.

Once again, Henry waited near the entrance to the room, playing a slot machine. If Fred saw him, it would not stand out. It was very common for slot players to continuously play a machine, believing that it was the "next" spin that wins. To give up a machine was uncommon for most gamblers because if someone does win, it only meant that it was because they "had warmed it up" and it was ready to yield the big win. Because of that mentality, Henry sitting at a slot for hours was not unusual.

When the card game ended, the comments indicated that Fred used tonight to give back some of the money to give them hope that his returning the next day was not necessarily going to be a winning streak. Little did they know, but that's exactly what Fred had in mind.

Fred thought, "*I lost tonight, as I wanted. The guys will think that the win streak tomorrow will not last. But yes, it will. Tomorrow night, I clean the table.*"

Henry watched Fred head back to his room. Time for Henry to do the same.

CHAPTER FIVE
Tuesday

Washington, DC

Frank Stone had returned to the home office. Sarah Castle also came back and was at the FBI building with Frank. They had interviewed many people, and brought back items for analysis at the FBI lab.

Frank started the meeting. "I cannot rule out terrorism. There were about 10 people who saw three people in thawbs and taqiyahs walking away from the humanities building at a very deliberate pace. No one remembers their faces, just their attire and their focused walk as a group."

"Frank, I'm not sure you're right. It could have been a ruse to throw us off. What would a terrorist want with these unique devices?" asked Sarah.

"Sarah, remember, I still don't know what is missing," complained Frank.

"Ok, let's go with the facts you have."

"Fine. We are now searching our databases on known terrorists and their locations. One of the perpetrators was about 6'1" to 6'3". That's unusual, so it should reduce the candidates."

"How do you do that?" asked Sarah.

"The NSA does help us with tracking all known terrorists worldwide. The new supercomputer can pinpoint on a map at any time those who are on the list. The ones who are still overseas we can eliminate. It's the ones in the USA that create a challenge. The NSA is limited in what they can do within our borders—or actually admit to doing."

"How do you track them?" asked Sarah.

"There are a variety of ways. The simplest is their known cell phones. However, some realize we do that, and have bought the new Off the Grid cell phone cases from US Tech Corp. The cases are a Faraday cage to block all radiation. Therefore, no pinging off cell towers. Another is facial recognition, and the variety of cameras monitoring traffic, public buildings, and private security monitors."

They had spent the last two days trying to determine who was near upstate New York while their cell phone was off the grid, then examine what candidates met the physical descriptions of the witness composites. It was not yielding many leads.

The terrorist leads were drying up fast. Nothing on the chatter that NSA retrieved showed anything having to do with upstate New York.

At that moment, Sarah got a call from Ralph Winston.

"Yes, Mr. Winston," she responded to his incoming call.

"Sarah, you're working with Frank Stone of the FBI on this project. Is that true?" inquired Ralph.

"Yes, sir. That's the situation," replied Sarah.

"Well, I have news that can help you, and then you and Frank can also help. Has Frank been read into this project?" continued the former president.

"No, sir. He has not," answered Sarah.

"This does not surprise me. I talked with Paul Sessions about the situation, but he still does not see the need to bring the right people into the loop. Since you're cleared, you need to deal with Reece Stanton on this," continued Ralph.

"I know Reece. We worked together years ago. He is also the assistant to Professor Quinn."

"Yes, he is, and more."

"How so, sir?"

"Reece was in a special group of talented agents that were cleared for assassinations.

They were strictly off the books and reported directly to me."

"Heavy duty here, sir. I do believe that's way above my pay grade."

"Yes, but because of his special skills and his old associates, they have already identified the perpetrators and are following them."

"That's way ahead of us, sir," commented Sarah. "How can we help, and what can we share?"

"Reece and his team will try to intercept these people. When they do, they will need recognized law enforcement to take over. You need to let Frank Stone know about Reece, but cannot let him know about Reece's prior history or how they are following the perpetrators. To do so would expose them to formal channels and blow their cover," clarified Ralph.

"Frank and I have been working without his being read into this program. He and I have established as much trust as we can without full disclosure. However, can you talk to him directly to help me on this?" asked Sarah.

"Absolutely," replied the former president.

Sarah then called Frank Stone over and handed him her phone.

"Who is it?" asked Frank as he took the phone. "Hello?" answered Frank with some reservations.

"Hello, Frank. This is Ralph Winston."

"Hello, sir. It's a pleasure to talk with you," replied Frank, with full sincerity and surprise.

"Frank, the project you're working on is full of classified information and more questions than answers. Unfortunately, the new administration is still keeping you in the dark, and I no longer have the authority to fully bring you into the situation. However, I'm able, through Sarah, to communicate additional information that will help you. You in turn can help her," informed Ralph.

"OK, how so, sir?"

"There is an off-the-record group of US agents who at one time reported directly to me. They have identified the perpetrators of your investigation. Our team leader actually worked on the items that were stolen. He is extremely resourceful and capable. His name is Reece Stanton."

"Wow, they have found the people who actually stole the items and exploded the bomb?" asked Frank.

"Yes, they have."

"They must be good; no, VERY good."

"The best, in my book," replied Ralph.

"Ok, how can we help?" asked Frank.

"Now recognize that I'm the former president, and don't officially have an actual role. However, I do know all the parties and can get you together to execute what needs to be done. Reece and his team do believe the terrorists are foreign nationals, and will of course try to leave the US. Our guys will try to intercept them while they're still in the US. If they do, they will need you to immediately take control of the perpetrators and provide cover for the retention of those people," continued the former president.

"When and where is this going to happen?" asked Frank.

"I don't know," responded Ralph.

"Ok, how will we know?"

"I'll get Sarah in contact with Reece so she can supply that information. Can you give me back to Sarah? Oh, Frank, thank you for working under such strange circumstances."

"It's an honor to talk with you, sir. Here she is," Frank said as he handed the phone back to Sarah.

"Yes, sir," answered Sarah.

"Sarah, I'll have Reece Stanton contact you so you and Frank can provide official control of the perpetrators when they intercept them. I'm not sure how they will do it and what condition the perpetrators will be in. According to the information Reece has given me, the three individuals are all part of the Ministry of State Security in China. That's the equivalent of the KGB. They are very dangerous, and with the hearing devices, they will present an existential challenge to capture. Reece is extremely resourceful. However, it may not be certain that he can apprehend the targets without killing them or causing a serious commotion. You and Frank will have to take over from there. It may be a mess, but the mission will be accomplished. Reece and his team never fail. Do you understand?"

"Yes, I do, sir. We'll be ready," replied Sarah.

Ralph then gave Sarah his secure phone number.

"Thanks. Goodbye and good luck." Ralph signed off.

Frank said to Sarah after she hung up, "Are you on a first-name basis with the pope? Should I expect a call from him this afternoon?" joked Frank. "Seriously, Sarah, the current and former presidents in one week. That's so far above my pay grade. How do you do it so casually?" said Frank in wonder.

"Frank, I told you this project was at the highest levels and has significant implications. Former president Winston said Reece would be calling me. I'll see if we can get into the loop so we can respond as quickly as possible."

Aberdeen, Maryland

Aberdeen, Maryland, was the location was one of the major military sites for developing and testing of a variety of military armament needs. There were test buildings for testing weapons from .22 caliber ammunition to 105 mm guns. The targets were set up to determine sabot designs and penetrating armor rounds. Some designs used a second round to penetrate a deflecting layer, such as a tank skirt. State-of-the-art weapons were one of the most important functions of the dedicated people who worked on the Grounds, which was the size of a small city. They had their own police force, as well as their own services to make it a community. People on the base were proud of what they did there and they did it well.

Slim pulled his garbage truck up to the MacDonald's back area where there was a large trash bin. It did not look out of place, except this was not one of his regular pickup times at this site. As he approached the area, three men came up in coveralls looking like they were part of his crew when he had helpers.

"Slim, we are your helpers today," the short person told Slim with authority.

"OK, what are you going to do?"

"We'll go with you and when we are done, we'll come back here after you're off the base."

The second person reached under the fender and pulled a lever. The modified door opened and revealed a small compartment that would be roomy for the three people inside. From the outside, the truck did not appear to be any different from the normal trash truck.

"When we want to get out, you will see a light come on the dashboard indicating overhead condition," instructed the short person. "When that happens, just stop what you're doing and we'll do what we have to do." The compartment had a camera system to observe everything around the truck. Inside, the "helpers" could watch where they were and if anyone was nearby.

"Ok," agreed Slim.

They climbed in and told Slim to go to the Grounds as he normally would.

As Slim approached, he was afraid the guards would ask to examine his modified truck. However, since he came on a routine run, there was no reason to question Slim or where he was going while on the base. After seven stops and trash pickups, he got the light signal at the eighth stop that there was overheating in the trash section. That was his signal. He then stopped the truck. He watched out the side mirror and saw the three passengers exit the truck and go into the building. This was an R&D building that rarely had a lot of material for pickup. After about 15 minutes, the three men exited the building with a tube about four feet long. They put the tube into the modified compartment and got into it as well.

Slim still had another nine stops. He completed those stops and drove off the base. He waved to the guard as he normally did.

He was still not happy having to be involved with some unknown people, but they had the leverage. His family was in jeopardy if he did not do what was asked of him. Slim pulled into the McDonald's parking lot and went to the trash area again.

He stopped and watched the access door open. Out poured the three men and the tube they got from the base.

They closed the door and put the tube in their SUV.

"Slim, remember, this never happened," admonished the short person.

"I understand," replied Slim.

Turning Stone
Tuesday Noon

Jeff had watched his target, Peter Huang, since he came out of the EPC room on Sunday night. Peter's routine was to get up late, have a leisurely lunch, go to his room, and come out for a fine dinner with wine about 7:00 p.m., then head to the Elite Poker Club room until midnight or 1:00 a.m., like last night. This morning he was up earlier and had a short lunch. Jeff watched Peter come down to the lobby. The target was checking out and leaving. He wasn't certain if he could take him now. There were too many people around; it could be dangerous.

"Please arrange for someone to wire my winnings to this account for me," Peter instructed the concierge while handing him a slip of paper with account details.

"Yes, sir. I can do that. It will take about 30 minutes," replied the concierge.

"That will be acceptable. I'll be in the restaurant having lunch," responded Peter.

After Peter received his wire transfer receipt he confirmed its transfer into his Cayman account on his iPhone. *"It really is comforting to know that this phone is secure and no one can open it except me. If Apple had given in to the FBI on the San Bernardino case, they could find out about my account. Good thing Apple prevailed,"* thought Peter.

Jeff saw Peter smile in satisfaction. Jeff realized that he wanted to know what was on Peter's mind, and wished he had the device and not Peter. Jeff now realized that obtaining the phone would also be important.

"My flight is not until tomorrow morning but I have to be on that flight at 9:50. The flights may be shut down on Thursday. By that time all hell will be let loose and I'll be in Taiwan. Away from the long arm of the US government or anyone else after me," thought

Peter while smiling his satisfaction. His plan was working. He was personally $15 million richer due to his bonus. *"I'm pleased that capitalism came to the Ministry of State Security (MSS) in China. Why should all of the other people of my country benefit from their labors and not me?"*

When Peter left his table from lunch, Jeff went to his table and retrieved his glass by putting it carefully into a bag. More to do tonight.

After his lunch, Peter had his car brought to him. He got in the car and proceeded to drive on the Thruway toward Syracuse. Jeff knew this was going to happen and had in anticipation got his car and was waiting for Peter to leave. Jeff reported in to Greg that they were on the move. Greg told Jeff that Peter had a reservation for a Delta flight out the next morning to Taipei, Taiwan. There was a layover in Detroit. They got Reece into a three-way call on how to proceed. Once Peter was out of the country, the situation got stickier.

Reece started the conversation. "Once Peter is out of the country, his status as a member of the Ministry of State Security (MSS) in China becomes an international problem for us. Our intercepting him becomes more than we want to deal with. Greg, you said his flight out of Syracuse was to Detroit and then a straight shot from Detroit to Taipei?"

"Actually, there is a layover in Narita between Detroit and Taipei," replied Greg.

"If we are to get him here in the US, it has to be either in Syracuse or Detroit," stated Reece.

"Did we get our support yet?" asked Jeff.

"Not yet. I expect a call anytime soon. We'll have to take action no matter what," answered Reece.

Jeff followed Fred to the Airport Inn at the airport grounds. It was not a fancy facility but it made up for it in its location. It was literally on the airport grounds. Jeff had to be nearby but not at the same hotel. There was a nice hotel on the corner of Col. Eileen Collins Blvd, which led into the airport, and South Bay Road. That's where Jeff went for the night. Jeff was depending on Greg to make sure that Fred did not change his reservation the next morning. Before turning in, Jeff took the kit from his bag and processed Peter's drinking glass. He then sent the results to Greg.

Idaho

Former president Winston now had to close the information and control loop. He had an extremely capable team chasing an equally dangerous team of foreign nationals in our country with a set of very secret devices. He knew Reece would be successful, and now he had to cover his back. During all of this, he was not in an official capacity. He was the *former* president, not the current president.

He called Reece. "Hello, Reece. I have taken action on your request. I have talked with Agent Sarah Castle. She is on this project officially, and also working with the FBI agent in charge of the explosion investigation. They will cover your back."

"Thank you, sir," replied Reece.

"Call Sarah and keep her in the information loop. She will arrange for backup and cleanup coverage as soon as she can when you take action. Hopefully this all can happen in the

USA. Here is her secure phone number," said Winston, and then gave Sarah Castle's secure phone number to him.

"I hope so too, sir. However, you know I'll follow them to wherever they go and complete my mission," explained Reece.

"I would expect nothing less from you, Reece. Now good luck," signed off the former president.

Washington, DC

Reece was still on the trail of his target, wondering what this third target was doing. He met with a person at the DuPont Circle Hotel and then he lost him in traffic and Greg could not find him. After hearing from former president Winston, Reece called Sarah Castle.

"Hello, Agent Castle. This is Reece Stanton. I'm on a secure phone. I'm assuming that the number former president Winston gave me for you is also secure. Is it?" said Reece.

"Hello, Reece. Yes, it is. What is the status?"

Reece told her about the location and activities of the two they had in coverage. Both had to be testing the devices and making money. The one in upstate New York was on his way to the Syracuse area. Reece said he had a flight out to Taipei the next morning. They agreed that they had to have coverage in both Syracuse and Detroit. Jeff was going to make the capture in either location, in the airport. In all probability it would be in the TSA-cleared sections of the airport, to confirm the target does not have a weapon for defense. They discussed the method of intercept and what to expect. As soon as it went down, Jeff would use a password to identify himself as a good guy. The FBI should nearby to move in officially. Reece gave Sarah the flight details so they could be prepared in either airport to come in as fast as the cavalry can.

Reece did not have current information on the target in Las Vegas. Since it was three hours' time difference, the target may not have made his move yet. However, Reece guessed that his departure would also be on Wednesday. This would be a challenge. There were a variety of flight options. There was a Korean Airlines direct flight from Las Vegas (LAS) to Seoul (ICN). If the perpetrator was on that flight, it would only be at McCarran International that they could make a US capture. Greg would have to search for flight reservations. Those flights were late at night and cut into their time for the poker games. There was a mid-morning Delta flight that put both the Turning Stone and Las Vegas targets on the same flight from Narita (NRT) to Taipei (TPE). If they did that, it would be impossible to intercept two at once. They hoped that wasn't the case. However, if their strategy was to take different flights to increase the chances of one getting away, they would not be on the same flight at any time.

Las Vegas

Fred was quite excited about his poker game tonight. He knew that with the hearing device, he was going to win. Yes, sometimes you don't get the cards. But when you did, it was like child's play. He had lost some $3 million last night, and was going for the full table tonight. The strategy was like Sunday night. Win and lose and then win. Eventually, it was all his.

As the night wore on, Fred was not getting the cards. Yes, there was luck involved. The games usually went to midnight or 1:00 a.m. At eleven o'clock, he was only up to $8 million. He was feeling the pressure to make it happen by 1:00 a.m. If someone who had lost most of their table stake wanted to quit at midnight, it would start a run of everyone quitting early to limit their losses.

Meanwhile, Henry was at another slot machine watching the poker room entrance.

He was sure that Fred was not going to leave early or skip the hotel. He had yet to hear from Greg about any flight arrangements. Reece was pretty certain that this was the last night. His guess was that the two gambling perpetrators were earning a bonus and had a deadline to leave the country. The sticky part was Reece's target. He was still in Washington. Reece had checked into the DuPont Circle Hotel to see if his target, James Wang, was still there. Greg said the hotel still had him as a guest. This one was strange.

At about 1:00 a.m., Fred came out of the poker game laughing and smiling, his fellow players telling him that he had to promise to be there again the next night to repeat his losing streak from the previous night.

Fred and Henry then went to their respective rooms for the night. Tomorrow was another day. What it would bring was truly unknown.

CHAPTER SIX
Wednesday

Baltimore

The harbor had been a showplace for tourists for a number of years in the revival of the city. The harbor also served as a crime dumping ground. Today was not going to be any different. It was early in the morning, and the air in the Baltimore/Washington area was crisp for this town.

"Hi, Slim," greeted Slim's short rider from the day before.

"I was told that this was the only thing I had to do for you. Please, leave me alone," pleaded Slim.

"Slim, we have a loose end to take care of first," smiled the short man. He then pulled out a Taser and put it to Slim's chest. It was a precise motion that caused even Slim's large size to fall in a matter of seconds. The short man was helped in putting Slim into the SUV. His size was normally a challenge, but not for these two men, who were physically fit and lifted Slim with ease.

They drove down to the harbor's water's edge to make the day's crime contribution. At least this was not a death by the Second Amendment target, the gun. It would not be a reason for extra attention. His pockets were loaded with some drug bags and a wad of rolled money, about three thousand dollars. A drug deal gone bad was not something that was out of the ordinary for a major city. They put Slim in the driver's seat in his dump truck that was on the barge at the harbor's edge.

Slowly the barge was moved to deeper water. After about 15 minutes, the truck was started. The helper lowered the window, put the truck into gear, and quickly exited the truck while closing the door as it slowly moved to the open edge of the barge. In a matter of moments the garbage truck was burping the air from the interior sections that either held trash or garbage or a driver. Slim was not conscious, and would not wake up. "*A garbage truck is better than the cement shoes of years past. No accidental floating back to the surface,*" thought the short man.

The short man then drove off to meet his contact again at the DuPont Circle Hotel.

Once at the meeting place, James answered the question about the loose end.

"Not a problem. Please take care of his dealer for me this afternoon before he finds out about Slim. Then we are clear."

"I can do that. Do you want it by gun or drugs?" his contact asked.

"Make it a drug deal gone bad. Make it a gun with some drugs spilled on site," clarified James.

"Did you find out about the time for the departure from the White House tomorrow?" asked James.

"Yes, about 10:00 a.m. The usual security measures will be taken regarding the actual car to be used for The Robin, the code name for Vice President Emily Spring. You can be located near the exit to determine which vehicle is the correct one. We'll have the team down further on Pennsylvania Avenue to intercept," replied the contact.

"We also need that modified garbage truck to be in the Potomac River later today. Can you arrange that?" questioned James to the contact.

"I knew that was a loose end and it was done with Slim," replied the contact, very proud of his taking the initiative. He had heard that Mr. Wang always took care of team members who did their jobs well. He also had heard of the fate of those who let him down. That was not so good, but was a lesson for everyone else.

Tomorrow was going to be a big day. When James came into the lobby, his normally observant eyes did not see the man sitting with a cup of coffee and reading the paper watching him. Reece once again had eyes on his target.

Pentagon

The command for new and advanced weapons was in panic. They'd discovered a new shoulder launched missile was unaccounted for as of last night. It had been in a secure facility that was impenetrable. Somehow, it could not be found. It had not gone out on the test range to be tested.

"General Binder, please tell me that the new anti-tank weapon was found in the men's bathroom!" yelled his superior, Lieutenant General Brian Rest.

"No, sir, it was not," responded Major General Binder.

"Then where is it?" barked Lieutenant General Rest.

"Sir, it was in its test location first thing Tuesday morning at 0800. It was not there when the crew that was to fire it came at 1100," informed Major General Binder.

"Who had access to that area?" asked Lieutenant General Rest.

"Sir, the only vehicle that came near the building that day was the normal garbage pickup. It was the normal operator, and nothing was out of the ordinary," explained Major General Binder.

"This is a priority. That weapon is the most advanced we have. It can penetrate almost any armament we have—or anyone, for that matter. As you know, once it penetrates it then explodes to destroy its target from the inside out. It's the personal bunker buster, if I need to remind you!" Again Lieutenant General Rest was screaming.

"Yes, sir. We are trying to locate the driver and his truck," responded Major General Binder.

"You're excused," said Lieutenant General Rest.

Major General Binder then saluted and left to pursue the missing weapon and the lead of the garbage service people.

Syracuse

Because Jeff knew that his target was scheduled to be on the Delta flight to Detroit, he went to the airport before his target. It was better to be there ahead of time, to not be detected, and perhaps be in a position to intercept him. The flight departure time was around 6:00 a.m.

Jeff expected a bit of inquiry by the TSA on his capture kit. He separated the items so they did not look like what they were. The injection systems were in a Meridian auto-injector system. The EpiPen is a well-known delivery system for anyone who has the need for immediate relief of life-threatening allergic reactions. Meridian makes this injection system. The TSA agent did not give it a second look. The plastic cable ties looked like any other way to tie things together. The special Buffalo Bill hat was a bit unusual. The x-ray showed a mesh in the top. Jeff explained that it was a special hat his brother had made for him so he would not crush it and ruin it. This was Buffalo Bill territory, so it got a pass.

Jeff sat down in the open area near the gate. His first impression was too much room and not enough people. There was not a way he could come up to the target and take him down here. It was going to be clumsy to do it here. He called Greg and told him that a Syracuse intercept was out. If he did it here, it may have to become lethal. They wanted to capture him, interrogate him, and get him out of the public as soon as possible. They agreed that Detroit was the place to do it. There was a long layover. Since it was an international flight, there would be more people pushing and moving. There was something about international flights that made people less attentive to their surroundings. That's what Jeff now had to hope for.

Reece got into the conversation and said that this would be good, since the boarding time for the flight from Las Vegas would preclude any communication to the projected capture time in Detroit. With a departure time around noon in Detroit, they would be boarding around 11:00 a.m. It would be 8:00 a.m. in Las Vegas and Los Angeles. Greg said that late last night, a reservation for Fred Tsim showed up on the Delta flight from Las Vegas to Taipei through Los Angeles and then Narita. The flight from Las Vegas did not land until 8:00 a.m. No chance for direct communication between those two. They were going to be on the same flight from Narita to Taipei. Reece thought that to be out of most team protocols. They couldn't intercept two on one flight. Perhaps that was their plan after all. Detroit must work.

When Peter entered the gate area, Jeff tried to be as inconspicuous as possible. He had to bump into him in Detroit to succeed. His training would remember all the people around him and not permit someone from another city to approach so close. Therefore, he had to blend into the limited background. Oh, how Jeff wished that Syracuse had a bigger crowd waiting for this flight! Greg did check what seat Peter was assigned. Then Greg obtained one closer to the front for Jeff so he did not pass by Peter, and then Peter would not see him as a Syracuse passenger when in Detroit. Not that some people don't take international flights from the same city. However, Jeff was certain that Peter was too well-trained to permit this to be a coincidence.

Jeff let Peter get on the plane first, then after many passengers, he got on and sat down as fast as he could. Unfortunately, his Buffalo Bills hat did make him stand out. Then Jeff noticed a man get on the plane with a Buffalo Bills windbreaker. *"Oh, thank you,"* thought

Jeff. As soon as he got settled, Jeff took off his hat and put the earphones in his ears to listen to music. Reece said this would distract his mind and confuse his perceived thinking in the event that his target was wearing the hearing device.

Las Vegas

Greg had contacted Henry and told him that he was on the same flight to Los Angeles as his target. The flight left at about 6:00 a.m. He behaved just like Jeff, at almost the same time he was boarding and avoiding his target. His hat was a Denver Broncos model. He also plugged into the music to distract his mind. He had to intercept at the LAX airport to be successful. The flight was full, so it was not hard for Henry to be lost in the crowd. Besides, Fred was as happy as Peter was with their winnings. He, like Peter, had set up a Cayman Island account. It was out of Chinese control and totally in his control. He had a good life with the Ministry, but he was ready to live without pollution, people, and filth. After he made the transfer, he was going to retire.

The flight was short, at a little over one hour. It was showtime for Henry when they landed. While in flight, Jeff planned what he should do for his move.

Detroit Airport

During the flight of one and a half hours, Jeff thought about how he was going to be successful. As anyone knows, on international flights, the planes are big. The crowds are anxious to get onboard. People crowd one another. There were accidental bumpings and movements. Jeff was depending on this situation to permit him to get close. He needed to wear his Buffalo Bills hat. The mesh inside masked his thought waves and made his target less able to perceive what he was thinking. As he made his way to the gate, he called Greg and told him the gate number and that he was going into action. Greg laughed, "Of course, I know what gate your flight departs from!"

This also made Jeff realize that he had to mask his thoughts further. He had to train his muscles to work as an image rather than a specific thought of words. That was a technique that Reece had told him to do to again obfuscate his thinking. Images don't translate. Therefore, he thought of it as a matador is piercing a passing bull, as in a bullfight.

As people gathered for the boarding process, he noticed that his target was going to board with the business class group. *"Oh no! Less people, less bumping, less anxious. They knew they had seats, they knew they had room for their carry-on baggage."*

It was now or never. The matador approached the bull. His auto-injection pen poised firmly in his hand would deliver the blow to bring down the bull. As he approached the bull, a child screamed to his left. The bull was distracted, but the bullfighter was not.

In one firm fluid upward motion, the auto-injection pen filled with the right amount of succinylcholine pierced the target's leg and immediately caused him to collapse.

Succinylcholine can kill if given in sufficient doses. This auto-injection pen had just enough to incapacitate the target. His muscles almost immediately went out of control. His reflex was not to defend but to put his hands in his pockets. Jeff had to put the breathing tube down his throat so he would not be so relaxed that he could not breathe. He quickly did that as he guided his body to the floor. People moved aside, realizing that someone was in need of help. Jeff removed Peter's hands from his pockets. It was then he discovered that the pockets had packets of acid that were burning off Peter's fingertips.

Jeff covered the hands with a handkerchief and secured his arms with the tie wraps. Again, in a fluid motion, Jeff had his phone out, speed-dialing to Greg. "Bring in the cavalry now," said Jeff. Within 30 seconds, six people with FBI in yellow on their jackets appeared and assisted Jeff. Jeff told the one in charge, "Applesauce." That was the code word telling the agent that he was the good guy and to help him. They picked up the target and carried him to the awaiting golf cart. The entire scene was cleared within seven minutes. The crowd was at first very quiet when the FBI showed up en masse. After the man who collapse was loaded onto the golf cart, the noise level went up dramatically. Everyone was wondering what he or she just witnessed. No one was around to ask. As fast as the FBI was there, they were gone.

They drove everyone to a holding area the FBI had arranged just off the concourse. Jeff carefully went through Peter's pockets and found his iPhone. They wanted to retrieve his information. That's why he burned his fingers. His phone was now of limited use. This was just like San Bernardino. Jeff called Reece and told him. Reece said don't worry. There was another way to get into the phone besides the code.

"Got the iPhone," Jeff told Greg.

"Give it to the FBI agent in charge. He will get it to me today."

"How are you going to get into it? You don't know his code and he destroyed his fingertips."

"Jeff, remember, you got his fingerprints from the glass. Well, with 3-D printing, I can make his fingertip and open his iPhone," answered Greg.

"Why didn't the FBI think of that for the San Bernardino case?" asked Jeff.

"They think too classically. No one thinks outside of the box. Make sure the phone is not shut down," quipped Greg. "We need to know what this guy has done and who he has communicated with recently. Oh, and, Jeff . . . great job! Now remove the hearing device. Put the device in your ear and talk to him. Then give him the second auto-injection pen," continued Greg.

"Will do," replied Jeff.

"One down and two more to go," thought Jeff.

Jeff took out the hearing device removal string. He pulled on it so the device was no longer in the ear of Peter. He cleaned it, and then inserted it into his own ear. Suddenly, life was a little different.

He went over to Peter, who was complete immobilized due to the sux shot. It would wear off soon, so he had to give him the immobilization shot and the knock-out shot.

"Ok, where was your final destination?" Jeff asked Peter. "Who hired you? Where will you turn over this unit? What is James Wang up to in Washington?"

The FBI agents stood in shock as this was happening. *"How could a man who got a sux shot talk? He was paralyzed,"* they all thought.

"Hong Kong, but I won't tell you that. We are freelancing. I don't know the client. What James is doing is something you will find out about tomorrow. You will be surprised. So will the vice president. Your country will be in shock tomorrow."

Jeff realized that he had enough information to help Reece and the team. They had to intercept before Hong Kong. If not here, then Taiwan. He also realized that the current administration had to be told to be on alert to protect the vice president.

Jeff then called both Greg and Reece. "They are heading to Hong Kong. Taiwan is a meeting point. I can't get specifics, but the vice president is in jeopardy. You have to pass that on to the administration," said Jeff, relaying what he had learned.

Reece first commented back, "That would explain why James Wang is in Washington. I wonder what they have planned. Do you know when this is going to happen?"

"Yes, tomorrow. He said the country will be in shock tomorrow," responded Jeff.

"That would explain why the two are leaving today. By tomorrow, both would have been in Taipei. Theoretically out of our reach," observed Greg. "Maybe it will be on the iPhone. Tonight we should be into it."

"Put him out with the benzodiazepine injector. We do need him to be aware of what we know and where he is going. The FBI will bring him to Washington on a special flight," said Reece.

"Will do," replied Jeff.

"Jeff, now put the hearing device in your secure box and use it later when you interrogate Peter." requested Reece. Reece realized that this was perhaps a mistake, but necessary. Jeff did too. He already realized it worked, and in the wrong hands, it was a weapon. Jeff had to be careful about handling this unit. This will be the only unit to survive because it was still in the US.

Los Angeles Airport (LAX)

LAX is one of the busiest airports in the world. When the flight from Las Vegas landed, Henry realized that he needed to find out the status of Detroit. When he turned on his iPhone on the taxi to the gate, he had a message: One down, two to go. *"Good news,"* he thought.

They had an almost three-hour layover. It was going to be tricky to keep track of his target, Fred, without being noticed. The Broncos cap did stand out in LA. The new Rams had not moved here yet but he was certain that loyalties had been established with the news of the pending move. LA was to have an NFL team again.

Fred was walking around the concourse, looking in shops and examining menus. Henry was trying to decide if Fred was doing this to determine if he had a tail. *"I wonder if Peter and he were to text or communicate before this flight. There was time to send a text and time to receive it. Perhaps the success of Detroit has put this target on alert. Greg said these guys were the best in the Ministry of State Security."* They did this for a living, and they were a match for Henry. But then Henry realized his training was every bit as good. At least he knew who his target was. At this point Fred may be on alert, but did not know who was following him.

Henry realized that following Fred for two hours was not a good idea. It was then that Henry got the brilliant idea to change hats. He started to visit shops with hats. He saw a variety of baseball caps. They should not be considered, for once they had been observed, they become memorable. He finally found a rain hat that was nondescript. It just flopped on and he was now Columbo. Henry removed the mesh in the Broncos hat and inserted it into the rain hat. He then considered also buying a new baseball cap. People wear baseball caps on planes, but not rain hats. A rain hat is appropriate for Taipei if they get there or in this airport prior to takeoff.

Henry had to strategize how he was going to get close enough while here. In his text messages, he was told how Jeff pulled off his interception. LAX is different, yet the same. People still crowd, but everyone moves more slowly. If he made a sudden move on the target, he would attract attention.

As it got close to the boarding time he noticed his target, Fred, was sitting down near the Priority Boarding carpet. As usual, there was cluster of other people near that carpet too. The announcement was made for families with children and the infirm to board. Next was Business Class. Fred moved quickly to his position to get onto the plane. He moved so quickly that Henry now realized that Fred must know they had intercepted Peter in

Detroit. Henry was not going to get an opportunity before they got on the plane. It was going to be the longest 12 hours Henry had ever lived. The question was whether to take the chance on the plane or do it in Narita. He had to know if backup was also on the plane. Time to text Greg.

"Cannot get to him in LAX. Is there backup on the plane for me?"

"I thought that would be the case. Working on it right now," Greg texted back.

"Boarding now. Do or die real soon," texted Henry. "Is it still American territory on US carriers over international waters?"

"Yes, it is. Don't do it over Japanese airspace. There may be a question about that," texted Greg.

"Can you get me moved up to Business Class? That's where he is. If I'm not there in an assigned seat, I'll stand out," texted Henry.

"I realized that too. Also working on that," texted Greg.

The boarding agent then announced, "Could Mr. Swenson come to the counter please?"

Henry heard his name and knew Greg had pulled it off somehow.

"Mr. Swenson?" asked the agent when Henry came forward.

"Yes," answered Henry.

"There was a computer glitch. Here is your proper boarding pass for Business Class," she politely said.

"Thank you," replied Henry as he then started to board with rest of the Business Class passengers. His target was probably already on the plane and settled in.

"Oh, Greg, you got me on. Now make it so I'm behind the target and I can watch and make my move," thought Henry.

Henry boarded the plane and found his seat at 12D. It was the last row on the starboard window. *"This is great. I'm behind Fred, and now I have to find him,"* thought Henry. Right after that thought, Greg came through with a text message. "He is in 3D."

"Thanks."

The lavatory was between Greg and Fred. His rain hat was probably not necessary for most of the flight. Since it was almost 12 hours to the stopover in Narita, he had time to plan the attack.

Then Henry thought it through and texted Greg. "Do I have backup on board?"

Greg texted, "Yes, trying to make contact at the highest levels I can so they will help you. Smitty is my best bet." Greg was referring to Jacob "Smitty" Smith, the current head of the FBI. He was holdover from Ralph Winston's administration. Smitty was about as straight a shooter as any person can be. He was also close to Ralph Winston. Henry figured they were enlisting Ralph to call Smitty and ask him to obtain the help. It had to be those guys who had the pull to get a US Marshal on board to expose himself to an unknown and support him. They would have to work out the details of the perpetrator custody when they landed in Japan.

"I may have my hands full and will have to do what I'm trained to do in the next 12 hours. Meanwhile Greg, Reece, and Ralph are going where no one has gone before to make this possible," thought Henry. *"Panic on a plane 36,000 feet in the sky is not a pleasant deal. It will have to be with as little commotion as possible."*

Henry went through the decision tree of the what ifs. After they are in the air, there will be drinks, a meal, people settle down for a video and some sleep. Some sleep and some are wide awake. Henry had to be prepared for

Fred to be on alert and wide awake. Henry decided the strategy had to be like every other passenger; have a drink, eat the meal, watch a video and then sleep.

Washington, DC

Greg got Peter's iPhone. He was impressed at how fast they were in getting it to him. He wasted no time using his 3-D printed finger with Peter's fingerprint on it to open the phone and gained access. "Bingo, it worked!" Greg yelled in delight.

He then checked the text messages. Suddenly, his heart sank. There was a text from Henry's target, Fred. It was, "I'm now in LA. Your flight to Detroit was on time. You were to confirm your flight status when you landed. Please confirm that you're still on your way." It was sent at 9:00 a.m. Pacific Time. It would have been received at noon in Detroit. Greg realized that at just before noon in Detroit they had captured Peter. It was now clear that Henry's target, Fred, was on high alert. He was really dangerous now. Henry was in a plane somewhere over the Pacific or the Yukon territories at this moment with a very dangerous man who knew his fellow agent had been compromised. In hindsight, they should have been prepared to open the phone and text back when they captured Peter.

Greg then called Reece.

"Hello, Greg. What's up?" answered Reece.

"Big trouble for Henry. Peter Huang's iPhone shows a text message from Henry's target indicating that he did not get an all-clear message from Peter when he was in Detroit. That would mean that Henry's guy is on full alert. Henry is walking into a bear's cave. We have to let him know in some way," explained Greg.

"You're right, it's bad. Tell you what; I'll contact Ralph Winston and see if Director Smith is onboard. I believe he should be, in order to clear the way for the Air Marshal to help Henry. Director Smith should be able to use the FAA communication system to talk with the pilot on the plane."

At 36,000 feet in a plane over the Yukon Territory

The passenger in seat 3D was a bit confused regarding the confirmation handoffs he and Peter had set. Fred thought, *"Peter is too good to be caught. Perhaps he missed the flight. Perhaps his phone was not working. Perhaps the cell system was down. Or, he was captured. If that's true, then I have to believe they know about me. Why not at the LAX airport or the LAS airport? There were plenty of opportunities to grab me. Am I that good? Well, I have to assume they have him, they know about me, and they will be waiting for me in Tokyo."*

The pilot was in the cruise sequence of the 12-hour flight. He had this run, back and forth, as his routine. To him it was a milk run, just a long one. In a couple hours his replacement would take the controls and he could relax. Then his copilot answered the FAA communication system.

"Yes, this is the copilot. How can I help you?"

"Jim, it's for you. It's FBI Director Smith,"

"Hello, this is Jim Watts, the pilot of Delta Flight 283," responded the pilot.

"Captain Watts, this is FBI Director Jacob Smith. I have some information for you, and a request for your assistance," Director Smith stated, getting to the point.

"How can I help?" asked the pilot.

"You have a special ops agent who reports directly to the president in seat 12D of your plane. His assignment is to apprehend a very dangerous foreign agent from the Ministry of State Security of China. This foreign agent is also on your airplane. Our guy will require the assistance of the Air Marshal in containing the foreign agent after apprehension. The man in seat 12D is named Henry Swenson. Please have the purser hand Mr. Swenson a note with the following information." Director Smith then dictated the message.

"Then have the purser arrange for the Air Marshal and Mr. Swenson to meet one another and coordinate their roles. Captain Watts, Mr. Swenson is a very skilled agent. He will accomplish his task without undue commotion or disruption. Upon your arrival in Tokyo, please don't let the Chinese agent leave the plane. As I understand international laws, the plane is your vessel and you're in command of it. It's US territory in this situation. It would complicate the situation to let him leave the plane. Do you understand everything I have told you?" continued Smitty.

"Yes, I do," answered Jim Watts.

"Thank you, Captain, and the president thanks you," replied Smitty as he hung up.

Then Jim Watts turned to his copilot. "Wow, this is not the normal milk run flight today!"

Jim then gave the information to his copilot and called Natalie Matins, the purser, and gave her the note and the instructions he had received.

As the passenger in seat 12D was settling in after the dinner and clean-up, the head flight attendant, also known as the purser, came to Henry and asked, "Mr. Swenson?"

"Yes," responded Henry.

"This is for you, sir," Natalie said, and handed him a piece of paper. Henry unfolded it and read the message.

"From Greg: Bad news. Target knows we have his friend. He will be on alert. Good news: you have a friend for backup in seat 5A. He expects you to make contact. Use the same flight attendant to arrange."

"Excuse me," Henry said to the purser as she started to leave.

"Could you please ask the passenger in seat 5A to meet me near the head over there?" he asked as he pointed to the lavatory in row area 10 behind the emergency exit space.

"Yes, sir," she responded.

Henry went to the lavatory area a couple rows forward when he saw someone enter it. As he got there a big man, probably 6'4", with blonde hair approached. *"This must be the Air Marshal, my backup,"* thought Henry.

"Hi, I'm Henry."

"I'm John."

"Have you been briefed?"

"Yes, except for the particulars and the timing," replied John Collie.

"It appears this head is occupied; I'm going to the one in coach," said Henry.

They both worked their way back to the set of lavatories just past the wing section of the plane. There was room in the exit area just aft of the lavatories.

"Navy?" asked John to Henry.

"Yes, how?" responded Henry.

"Heads are on ships," observed John.

"Just a habit. And you?" replied Henry.

"Jarhead."

"Still the same branch."

"Here is the situation and what I'm going to do."

Henry briefly laid out the plan based upon his target knowing that he was now known, and would be on high alert. They would use the purser to let John know when to move into position for immediate assistance after the take-down. The purser also had another special set of instructions for the pilot.

Idaho

Former president Winston now realized that his successor had not taken this situation seriously yet. It was time to call President Sessions and have him read FBI Director Jacob Smith and the Chairman of the Joint Chiefs of Staff (CJCS), General Daniel Broadtail, in on the Hearing Project, to be available to support Reece and his team.

"White House, how may I help you?" answered the White House operator.

"Hello, this is Ralph Winston. Can you pass me on to President Sessions, please?" answered former president Winston.

"Oh, hello, President Winston. I'll direct your call to his office. Nice talking with you, sir," replied the operator. Former president Winston was popular not only with the general public, but with anyone who came in contact with him. He had personally visited everyone at the White House while president.

This included the switchboard staff, the janitorial staff, and anyone else who made his period as president work.

"President Sessions' office," was the next answer.

"Hello, this is Ralph Winston. Is the president available?" asked Ralph. Although people often referred to him as President Winston or Mr. President, he never referred to himself as President Winston. He was the former president, not the current president, and technically Mr. Winston.

"Sir, as you know, his schedule is very busy. I'll let Mr. Edwards know you're asking for him," was the answer Ralph got.

"Thank you," replied Ralph.

Once again it was call and wait.

Ralph was called back from the White House within five minutes.

"Hello, Mr. Winston. This is Roger Edwards, sir. Can I tell the president the nature of this call?" was the greeting President Sessions' chief of staff gave to the former president.

"Yes, tell him it has to do with the Hearing Project," answered Ralph.

"Perhaps I can help you on that, sir," offered Mr. Edwards.

"Mr. Edwards, not unless you're able to extend POTUS eyes only clearance to an individual," retorted Ralph, now annoyed that he was being handed off to a chief of staff, a lightweight, in his opinion.

"No, I'm not permitted to do that. I assume you need to talk directly with President Sessions?" answered Roger Edwards, sensing the displeasure on the other end of the phone.

"Just a minute, Mr. President," continued Edwards.

The phone went dead for a minute. No music or other background sounds while on hold.

Two minutes later, "Hello, Ralph. How can I help you?" asked President Sessions.

"Paul, the situation on the stolen Hearing Project units is getting complicated for you. It's time for you to bring FBI Director Smith and Chairman of the Joint Chiefs of Staff (CJCS) General Broadtail in on this. Smitty has people working on retrieving the units without knowing what they are doing. I did step slightly over the line and asked Director Smith to help Reece Stanton in his effort. We now need to make sure there is full support for Reece," explained Ralph.

"Who authorized Reece Stanton to take any action?" questioned President Sessions, now upset that he was not totally in control.

"Paul, he developed the units, and knows how dangerous they are in the wrong hands. He took the initiative to locate the perpetrators and get the units back. Trust me, you will be pleased that Reece is in action for you," said

Ralph, without the least bit of apology in his voice.

"Dangerous, **IF** they work; how can dangerous can they be? Oh, read someone's mind on what wine he or she wants for dinner?" He was now mocking the former president for both the disbelief they worked or could pose any use that was dangerous.

"Paul, you and I may disagree about the units, but I believe that Reece Stanton's assessment on the potential danger is spot on. Remember, we developed them to obtain meaningful information from terrorists we captured without water boarding them," Ralph replied with confidence.

"OK, you want me to extend POTUS eyes only to FBI Director Smith and General Broadtail on this?" Sessions insolently answered.

"Yes, please do that. Oh, I have another request to ask to assist in this effort. Could you call General Broadtail and request that he take calls from Greg Mays and assist him in any way he can?" continued Ralph, not missing his successor's displeasure at being told what to do.

"As I'm the **CURRENT** president, will you please keep me in the loop?" retorted President Sessions with rancor.

"Absolutely," responded Ralph, trying not to laugh.

Ralph then proceeded to bring Sessions up to speed.

Ralph ended with what was prophetic, "Paul, I'm certain there will a calamity soon if we don't locate and capture these people. As I said, Reece is the best person to have on your team. Please don't get in his way."

After they got off the phone, President Sessions then called Director Smith to come to his office for a quick meeting.

Director Smith was there in 15 minutes and was read into the Hearing Project. Director Smith now knew how serious this whole situation was for the country.

Director Smith then called former president Winston and thanked him for untying his hands. Ralph was modest, and knew he should have done that while he was president. Ralph apologized to Smitty for this oversight.

Smitty now knew he had to do whatever was requested to make sure those units did not leave the US or continue to be out of their control.

President Sessions then called General Broadtail, Chairman of the Joint Chiefs of Staff (CJCS) for the military. He informed the general about the Hearing Project and to extend courtesies with support to Greg Mays and Reece Stanton. The general said he knew about Reece, and commented on Reece's skillset. President Sessions made a note to himself to meet and understand this amazing guy who was out there. It was Paul's opinion still that Reece was a rogue. He was the president, and should have control of this man and his actions. However, Paul realized that Winston was a good of judge of character, and he had to put aside his ego and let Reece do his thing.

Ralph Winston then called Greg Mays and told him that both FBI Director Smith and Chairman of the Joint Chiefs of Staff (CJCS) Broadtail were in on the team's effort.

"Greg, both Smitty and General Broadtail are not only on the team but are available to support you. Call them when you have a chance to open the lines of communication," stated Ralph.

Over the Pacific at 36,000 Feet
Flight from LAX to Narita Airport
(Tokyo, Japan)

Most of the passengers were quiet, with the lights low. They were about six hours into a 12-hour flight. The cabin had the lights low except for the night owls watching a video on the individual monitors, making it conducive for sleep. The Business Class seats were both window and aisle. The seats were laid out so passengers did not even notice other passengers.

Meanwhile, Henry was deep in thought. "*I have to act within the next couple of hours. Reece said this had to happen over international waters on a US carrier so it's still US soil. The guy in Detroit told the guys that something bad was going to happen tomorrow. He also referenced the vice president. I hope the guys back home have that covered. OK, time to rock and roll.*"

Henry rang his attendant button and then he stood up. He reset the button. The purser saw him get up and knew it was time for action. As Henry went forward in the plane he saw his target was fully awake with a blanket over himself. It would be impossible to use the auto-injection system in this situation and be certain of immobilizing Fred. As he got about three rows behind Fred, Henry pressed the trigger on the device Reece had given him. It was part of the antidote package.

Suddenly, Fred jumped from his seat and was clawing at his ear. The noise within his ear canal was debilitating. The screeching sound was making his eardrum hurt with so much sound and at a frequency that even the deaf could hear. As he removed the device, Fred noticed another passenger trying to get by him in the aisle. Fred was now out of breath and totally distracted. He did not even notice the sudden arm movement of this passenger to his upper arm as he bumped into him.

Henry had activated the antidote that caused the hearing device to activate a piercing sound in his ear that makes removable of the device an immediate action. Henry knew that Fred would not even notice him. As Henry moved by Fred, he moved his right hand swiftly to deliver the sux in the auto-injection system, while his left hand grabbed the hearing device now in Fred's hand.

Immediately, Fred went limp. Henry eased him down into the seat. As he was doing that, both the purser and John Collie were there to assist. They had to immobilize him with tie wraps. Henry inserted the small breathing tube so Fred could still breathe. Fred was not going to be interrogated with witnesses, so Henry delivered the other auto-injection system that delivered the benzodiazepine to knock him out. The purser then covered him with the blanket and went about her business as if nothing had happened. She then, as well as Henry, silently thanked Delta for having fully flat seats for flying in Business Class. She then called the pilot, Jim Watts, for him to relay back to the director of the FBI that they had been successful.

The only question now was what to do with the now asleep passenger. They still had hours to go, and many hours back home to the US.

Henry then returned to his seat and thought, *"Two down, one to go. Reece, it's your guy we now have to worry about. Who was behind all of this? We do have to find that out. Oh, well, now to catch a few z's."*

Henry pulled out the crusher box from his carryon. He put the hearing device in the box and closed it, thereby crushing it. He then took out the acid vial and put the crushed device into the vial. So much for advanced technology.

    With this last task, Henry then fell asleep, knowing the passenger in seat 3D was also asleep beyond his control.

CHAPTER SEVEN

Thursday

Narita Airport - Tokyo, Japan

The Delta flight landed as scheduled at about 2:45 p.m. local time. It was 13 hours ahead of Eastern Daylight Time (EDT) in the United States. Japan does not change its time for daylight savings, as is done in most of the US. It was 1:45 a.m. on the East Coast of the US.

The passengers deplaned, as is the normal routine when the plane lands at Narita on the layover to Taipei. The plane is refueled, cleaned, and inspected. Captain Jim Watts knew he would have to explain to the Japanese people that came on the plane why he was not getting off, as well as the Air Marshal, the purser, and two passengers. They had Delta communications place a call to FBI Director Smith. This was a difficult situation for Director Smith. They had captured a person on the flight because President

Winston had told him it was a critical action based upon Reece Stanton's recommendations. They then discussed how to handle the captured perpetrator.

Director Smith started the conversation, "Henry, I understand the background on the offense made by this man. It's necessary to not let this man off the airplane. Captain Watts, you have my full support to not release this man to the Japanese or anyone else."

Captain Jim Watts said, "That's going to be a problem, sir. This physical plane is scheduled to continue on to Taipei in about three and a half hours. We then spend the night there and fly the route back through Narita and then to Los Angeles, for an evening arrival on Friday. There will be a crew change in Taipei, so I won't be on the return flight. How do we proceed?"

"Once he comes off the plane, he has to be placed in the custody of the government there, be it Japan or Taiwan. That then creates a State Department situation that becomes caught in the diplomatic world," clarified Director Smith.

Reece came into the conversation. He had been asleep, but Greg woke him and got him tied into the conference call. It was the middle of the night on the US East Coast. They brought Reece up to speed on the status and the new challenge.

"Henry, great going on your successful intervention," said Reece. "Smitty, I think I have a solution to that, with a slight detour." Reece was very familiar with Director Smith from his years of reporting directly to President Winston. Having the FBI as protection in your back pocket helped a few times.

"Tell me what that creative mind of yours has for us," responded Director Smith.

"I have flown the trip from Narita to Taipei many times. I used to do it when the layover was Osaka, before Delta changed it to Narita. About halfway between Tokyo and Taipei is the island of Okinawa, with the Kadena Air Base. That's considered US property. The plane only has to land, and drop off Henry and his new best buddy. I would include the Air Marshal for good measure. It's almost on the flight path your commercial plane would take, Captain Watts. What I then recommend is for our esteemed Air Force to send everyone expeditiously back to the US. Director Smith, can you arrange that?" explained Reece.

"Wow, great idea. Let me see who at the Pentagon is up at this hour that I know. Captain, I need the contact information for Delta clearance to do this drop-off. You say I have three hours to pull this off?" answered Director Smith.

"Smitty, General Broadtail, Chairman of the Joint Chiefs of Staff, is on our team. Call him and ask him to help us," said Greg.

"Yes, sir. That's the schedule. If we can maintain that schedule, the company will be happy to work with the US government. We are a US-based airline," answered Captain Watts.

They agreed to the new plans and all hung up, waiting to hear from the success of cooperation of the Air Force and Delta Airlines.

Near the Kadena Air Force Base on the Island of Okinawa

It only took two hours to get the Pentagon to arrange the Delta flight to land at the Kadena Air Force Base. Delta stepped up as a good corporate citizen.

As they started their descent, Captain Watts came on the PA system. "This is Captain Watts. You will note we are in a descent before Taipei. We have a medical emergency that has happened to a customer on board. We'll shortly land at Kadena Air Force Base on the island of Okinawa. The stopover will not be long. We'll deplane the people we need to for this emergency and within 15 minutes be on our way again. Let me assure you that we can make up that time and have an on-time arrival at Taoyuan International Airport. Thank you in advance for your understanding."

The plane landed without incident. They brought a stretcher onboard to carry off Fred. He was still sedated. Fortunately, Henry had several auto-injection systems loaded with benzodiazepine. This will keep Fred in dream land until he gets to the states. The entire unloading took less than 10 minutes. Henry personally thanked Captain Watts and the purser.

"I'll look for you on my next Delta flight," Henry said with a wink.

The purser smiled back and said, "I'll be looking for you, too. Glad to help. Please, next time make it less exciting."

After everything was finished, the plane was pushed back and cleared for takeoff. The captain was spot on for the 15-minute layover estimate.

It was 7,666 miles as a straight shot from Okinawa to Washington, DC. There was a C32 available for transport back.

Unfortunately, the plane has a range of only 5,650 miles so it had to stop for refueling somewhere. They would have to stop at either Elmendorf Air Force Base in Alaska or Hickam Air Force Base in Hawaii en route. It was 4,679 to Hawaii and 4,827 miles from Hawaii to DC. It was 4,313 miles to Elmendorf and 3,445 miles from Elmendorf to DC. No question, 7,758 miles beats 9,506 miles. Since they were not leaving the plane for the beach, it was the northern route to Alaska that was chosen.

The C32 is the military version of the Boeing 757. It has a cruising speed of 605 mph. That means it would take about 13½ hours to make the trip, allowing for refueling. It was now 9:00 p.m. Thursday in Japan. The time in Washington was 8:00 a.m. Thursday. The layover in Elmendorf would be at about 3:30 p.m. in Washington.

Henry settled back to sleep during the seven-hour flight to Elmendorf. He was not jubilant, as he thought, "*I got my target, no one was hurt, and now we're headed back to the US. Time to sleep.*"

Washington, DC
FBI Headquarters

It was a hectic evening for Jeff. He had to contain his captive, Peter, and transfer him over to the FBI agent that showed up, Frank Stone. Fortunately, Jeff only had to show up the next morning. He was to be joined by Frank Stone, the lead terrorist investigator for the Northeast, and three of his agents. Jeff was surprised to find out that in the welcoming committee was a CIA agent, Sarah Castle. There was history with Sarah and Reece with the rescuing of a Senator's daughter a few years ago. On his way in to the Bureau, he called Greg to check in.

"Greg, I'm now in DC on the way to the Bureau. Frank Stone took charge of Peter Huang last night from me. What is the status on Henry?" said Jeff.

"Henry got his man on the flight before it got to Narita. They did not take him off the plane, so he never was in Japan for us to have to turn him over to the Japanese government," explained Greg.

"How is Henry getting the target back to the US?" asked Jeff.

"Reece came up with a brilliant idea. It was a bit of coordination at this end, but the Delta flight continued from Narita to Taipei with a short layover at Kadena Air Force Base on the island of Okinawa. It was on the way, with only about a two-hour flight," answered Greg.

"When do they get here?"

"The ETA is 8:30 tonight our time."

"We need to use the hearing device to interrogate my guy. I have the device, but I need to know who is cleared to know about it," questioned Jeff.

"That's still a sticky wicket. Frank Stone is the FBI guy in charge, and he has three agents also working with him. None of them, including Frank Stone, are read in on the program. Therefore, you cannot tell them what and how you're going to interrogate Peter. The good news is that the director of the FBI, Jacob Smith, is now cleared. You will also run into Agent Sarah Castle from the CIA. She is a techie who was assigned to the Hearing Project. So good luck. Ask for the director when you show up. I'm sure he can arrange for just you and Sarah to interrogate Peter Huang at some time," answered Greg.

It had been years since Jeff had been to the "new" FBI headquarters. It was 1975 when it was dedicated, and was to be replaced once politicians agreed on what was to be done. In the meantime, they had to work with what they had . . . a building closing in on a half-century, with more responsibilities than had ever been projected. Terrorism was only the start of the new tasks under their purview.

Jeff checked in and asked to be cleared for the director's office. The greeting person was surprised that someone off the street was so bold. She was equally surprised when Director Smith came on the line and instructed her that someone would be down to escort Mr. Jeff Harrison to his office.

Jeff waited about five minutes. The young lady, who had to be an agent anyone would like to be arrested by, showed up. Counter to her physical attractiveness, it was apparent that she was not one to be messed with. She professionally asked to see Jeff's ID and then took him up to the director's office. As they entered the suite, the director came out and greeted Jeff.

"Very good job, Mr. Harrison, on your take-down at the Detroit airport. Very few people knew what had happened. That's the way we like it. SSA Frank Stone is now with the perpetrator, Peter Huang. He knows that he is the target from the explosion and that there is a team working to find the other perpetrators. I have asked Frank to join us in a few minutes. I'm assuming you have the recovered hearing device. I'm also assuming that it would be best to interrogate him with you using it. It would conflict with protocol to displace Frank and have you be the lead interrogator. However, I'll explain to Frank that you will be there and assist in the direction of questioning. Are we clear? Oh, one more thing. There is a CIA agent, Sarah Castle, who is also in the group. She was the CIA techie on the Hearing Project and is therefore fully read in on the project. You can share with her aside all you need to. She has a good rapport with Frank."

"Understood," responded Jeff. As he said that, Frank Stone entered the office.

"Frank, this is Jeff Harrison, as you know from Detroit. Jeff, officially, this is SSA Frank Stone, the agent in charge of the investigation," said Director Smith.

"Frank, nice to officially meet you," greeted Jeff, extending a hand.

"My pleasure, Jeff. We need good guys like you. Glad we are on the same side," Frank cheerfully said while he grasped Jeff's hand and firmly shook it.

"OK, with the formal introductions made, let me structure some of this for you two so we can all play nicely. Frank, as you know, our perpetrator was one of the people responsible for the explosion on the college campus. He has another associate who was captured on a flight to Narita and is now on his way back here. There is a third person still on the loose but under surveillance. We have not had the opportunity to intercept him.

"Now this is where it gets a little sticky. The objects that the perpetrators stole were the results of an extremely secret project that was classified as POTUS eyes only. I was only recently read in on it myself. As you know,

Agent Sarah Castle was part of the development team. She therefore has clearance. Jeff is working with another person of the development team, Reece Stanton. I'm assuming that Jeff is privy to the details of the project. We do need to get information out of your new prisoner. I would like both Sarah and Jeff to assist you in the interrogation of the prisoner. They will have a dimension no one else can have. Can we do this?" explained Director Smith.

"Absolutely, sir. I already appreciate Agent Castle's mind," responded Agent Stone.

As Frank and Jeff approached the interrogation room, Jeff excused himself to privately confer with Sarah. Frank understood and let them be alone.

"Agent Castle, I have one of the devices. I'll put it in my ear to use it. Knowing how much you would like to try it, this afternoon we can trade off and you get to use it. Any problem with that proposal?" asked Jeff.

"That will work for me," responded Sarah.

Greg had let Director Smith know about the background of Peter Huang as a member of the Ministry of State Security (MSS) in China. As it was the Chinese version of the KGB, they knew they were in for a challenge.

Peter was in restraints, with handcuffs attached to a belt restraint and ankle shackles. He was not going anywhere. His acid-burned hands were now in gloves with salve inside. It was so unfortunate he did that to himself to prevent access to his iPhone. The FBI was one step ahead of him, with Reece's team's help.

It was a brightly illuminated. This was a technique to focus intensity onto the subject. Across the table were Frank and Jeff. Sarah was behind him, and the others where in chairs in the corner. His handcuffs through a U-bolt attached Peter to the table.

"We know who you are, Peter," started Frank. "I want to know who you were working with and what you were after when you created the chaos at the college campus."

Peter just smiled.

"If you had one of those devices you would be able obtain my answer. I think you broke it. Do you think I would tell you anything? I know your government will not permit water boarding or anything close to what you consider torture. In my country, we don't have those limits. Ha, such amateurs," thought Peter.

"I'll not tell you anything. I'm a tourist visiting your country. I had nothing to do with any colleges. I request access to my country's embassy," answered Peter.

Jeff then thought, *"Damn, this thing works. I hear him as if his lips were moving and he was talking."*

Jeff nodded to Sarah that he was getting the information they wanted.

Frank then continued asking questions, one after another.

"Who else was working with you? What are their names? You were on your way to Taiwan. Was that your final destination? Is there an all-clear signal that you're OK? Is there a time upon which you must signal everything is OK?"

As Frank ran through the questions, Peter was not aware that his thoughts were answering the questions, though with smug other thoughts about how they would not catch James. He was the ace in the hole.

Frank was told to just ask questions as if the guy was answering them. He continued. The session lasted about one hour. Then Jeff asked for a short break. It was now Sarah's turn to use the device. She had used a prototype during the development process but this is what it was developed to do… reality.

In the afternoon session, Sarah was very pleased with the capability of the Hearing Device. She almost found it a miracle that in the interrogation, the perpetrator was actually answering their questions. Wow, it was great.

Washington - Near DuPont Circle

This was going to be a very busy day for James. He got up, went down, and had breakfast. Then he called his contact and asked if they were in position. The team was ready. It was a twenty-minute walk from DuPont Circle to the entrance gate to the White House. By walking, James could monitor if he was being followed. He had not heard from Peter on his flights to Taipei. He could only believe that he was discovered. Obviously, it was important to accomplish his two tasks for the day. As he walked, he would back up and see if there was anyone who was standing out in the crowds. It was 9:00 a.m. Most people would be in their offices. It was a straight shot down Connecticut Avenue to Lafayette Square. Unfortunately, there were not a lot of store windows to stop and do the window-shopping observation for tails. When he crossed K Street, there was Farragut Park.

He would sit on a bench and determine if there was in reality anyone behind him. He did see a familiar face and did a nod. It was hard to not smile in confidence. Normally James did not have any anxiety, but today was something that would shock the US. It was different.

Reece observed James leaving the hotel restaurant after his breakfast. Like Jeff did at the Turning Stone restaurant, Reece casually walked by the table that James had used and had not been cleared yet. In one smooth movement he picked up the water glass, emptied the remaining water into the coffee cup, and inserted it into his plastic bag. He then headed to the subway station at DuPont Circle.

Reece had guessed that James was headed to the White House. The walk the other day was a dry run. Therefore, it was better to be ahead of him and not to appear to be a tail. He had to assume that James was aware of Peter's fate and was on alert too.

With the subway, Reece was at the Farragut Metro station in a matter of minutes. He then casually entered the park on the south end near Eye Street. When he saw James coming down to the park, Reece went ahead of him and crossed I Street, continuing down Connecticut Avenue toward Lafayette Park. Once again, Reece headed to the southernmost edge of this park and found a bench. He sipped his coffee and pulled out his *Washington Times* to appear to be reading.

Pennsylvania Avenue had been shut down for vehicular traffic for years as a safety precaution to the president and others. However, the White House still used the north entrance for egress.

After James was sure that no one was following him, he got up from his Farragut Square bench and headed to the location near the White House vehicle entrance. There was uniformed Secret Service everywhere. As he approached the officer who appeared to be directing the traffic from the White House, he asked if the vice president was just leaving. The officer told him that the vice president was in one of the five cars but could not tell him which one. The routine was to have several cars leave at the same time without anyone knowing which had the vice president aboard. All the cars headed in different directions once they exited the White House grounds.

"Robin in the third car," was in the message earpiece for the officer directing traffic. "Direct her down Jackson Place. She is to get onto Connecticut Ave then around DuPont Circle, and then take Massachusetts Avenue back to the Observatory," again he heard in the earpiece.

Meanwhile, the officer was reciting in his head the message. *"Third car, down Jackson Place along the park to Connecticut for the straight shot home."*

At this time, the pestering tourist left the White House gate area and called his contact. "It's the third car, going to Connecticut. Intercept at Farragut Square."

Reece observed James asking the Secret Service officer at the gate a couple of questions, like any other tourist. The camera around his neck was all part of his cover. After the cars started coming out, Reece saw James call someone and walk away from the gate area. He was now heading into Lafayette Park and doing the diagonal path toward the H Street and Madison corner. A block and a half from that corner was the McPherson Square Metro station on 15th Street. That had to be the destination for James. He had done what he had come to do and now was leaving as fast as he could.

Reece was in the center of the park on the southern edge. There was no direct path to cut off James. Once he was on the subway, it would be hard to find him without Greg's help. Reece decided that he could continue along Pennsylvania Avenue at a focused walk and then run up 15th Street while out of sight of James. He needed to get there before James.

Farragut Square
9:15 a.m.

James's helper was positioned on Farragut Square's southern edge that fronts on I Street as if he was taking pictures of the Washington buildings. Tourists and other people were forever doing things out of the norm while in the country's capital. It was their capital, and it was theirs to visit and remember, as they wanted to. The long housing for the tripod was on the ground and did not attract any special attention by the people in the park. It was about 10:15 a.m., after the commuters were at work; only the tourists were out on the streets of Washington.

Suddenly, several DC police cars drove quickly up Connecticut Avenue. They were the gauntlets of protection for the dignitaries who drove through this city without regard to traffic lights or other cars. Following the initial set of DC police cars were five large black SUVs with tinted windows. The tourists all stopped to wonder who was so important to have such an escort. As the third SUV crossed I Street on Connecticut Avenue, there was a loud hissing sound and a flash of light that came from the tube that was for the tripod.

In a matter of seconds, it was apparent that the tube has launched a missile toward the third car. The sound of contact was so loud that several people could not hear for several minutes, the ringing in their ears was so overwhelming. The car was prepared for such an attack. It could take most armaments, even anti-tank weapons, at close range. But this was no normal anti-tank missile. It was the missing new weapon from Aberdeen. It was the personal bunker buster. It not only penetrated targets, but once inside the target, it explodes with such energy that it was the shock and awe of great fame. It was awesome!

The formerly black SUV was in pieces flying through the air for several hundred feet. There were parts, probably the seats, flying on fire. If there was anyone inside, which there had to be, they most certainly did not survive. The other cars in the procession swerved to miss hitting what was left of the engine and frame of the former SUV. Chaos was now the theme of this quiet park. Small fires were scattered for 100 feet around where the SUV was hit. After the mind-numbing explosion, there was an eerie silence that filled the air. No voices, no traffic, no movement. The world at Farragut Square had stopped. It was a mind-capturing pause. It was surreal.

Then, as suddenly as it all happened, sirens filled the air, cars started moving, people began screaming. The smell of the destruction filled the air with the propellant of the bunker buster, the pungent smell of items that were either a part of the SUV or someone in the

SUV burning. All the people in the vicinity will never forget what they were involuntarily a part of today. All their senses were in play. There was sound, smell, sights, and the shock wave of the air blast. Those in the area heard, saw, smelled, and felt this memorable event.

The tourist who had been taking pictures immediately turned from the awful fireball and debris flying and ran toward the Farragut West Metro Station entrance on the corner of 17th Street and I Street. It was on that corner of the park. He was walking down the steps of the escalator to speed his descent into the Metro system. In a matter of moments he would be just another passenger on the Metro.

In a matter of five minutes there were several Secret Service SUVs and DC police cars blocking all traffic and trying to make sense of what had just occurred. The vice president, Emily Spring, had just been assassinated.

The McPherson Square Metro Station

Reece ran up 15th Street. When he was at H Street, he saw that James was ahead of him and on the escalator. He was getting away. Sure enough, when Reece got down the escalator, running down the steps as it went, he missed which way James was going. As Reece was at the top of the escalator he heard the loudest explosion he had heard since Iraq. It could have been a bunker buster impact, from his experience. He had heard two distinctly loud explosions. The first was penetration, and the second, within milliseconds, was the explosive element. This was what James was up to.

Reece called Greg and told him what had just occurred and that they had to find James. Reece then told Greg about the explosion and to monitor the government information sources. He was going to take the Metro back to his car and head north. His intuition was that James Wang was now headed out of the country. He had to find him and retrieve the hearing device.

James saw the man in pursuit of him. He somehow attracted attention and was now a person of interest for someone. *"I still have much to do before I leave this country. I'm certain the US government will do all they can do to make sure I don't leave the country. My plan will work; I'll get out with my reward,"* thought James Wang.

Reece then called Greg and told him he had lost James Wang in the Metro system. He asked Greg to find him. His first option was the Metro station at DuPont Circle, where James Wang had left his car. Meanwhile, Reece took the next train to DuPont Circle to retrieve his car.

Before Reece's train arrived at the DuPont Circle station, Greg called him.

"Reece, he did get off at the DuPont Circle station. I'll check the hotel security cameras and see if that's where he is headed," stated Greg.

"Thanks, Greg. I'll go there to get my car too. Let me know through traffic cams where he is headed," replied Reece.

Reece got his car and headed out of Washington as fast as he could. Although Washington had the letter streets that went east to west and the numbered street going north to south, the state streets cut at angles with many other streets, making other crossovers. Only in Washington do Missouri and New Hampshire intersect. Reece knew that to get to the capital loop and then onto Route 95 north, he had many options. He chose going on P Street east to 7th Street, which changes to Georgia as it proceeds north. Then on New Hampshire to the Beltway loop.

Reece was just crossing the Baltimore loop of Route 695 when he got a call from Greg.

"Reece, I found James. He is just heading into the Baltimore I-95 tunnel. He is about 30 minutes ahead of you. Do you know what you're going to do when you catch up to him?" said Greg.

"No, I do have to get close enough and then decide what my opportunity will be," replied Reece. "We cannot lose him again. He knows where he is headed and how to get there. I'm not going to underestimate him again."

"Hey buddy, just to let you know the explosion you saw was the assassination of the vice president. It is all over the news. Turn on your radio."

"Thanks. They are playing for keeps. I suspect James is ultimately headed to Taiwan. That was where both Fred and Peter, the other two perpetrators, were headed. Jeff is back from Detroit with Peter. Henry has captured

Fred Tsim. If my timeline is right, he is on a military flight from Kadena Air Force Base to Elmendorf."

"Do you know his ETA into Elmendorf?" asked Reece.

"Yes, it's to be 3:30 p.m. our time this afternoon. What are you thinking?" asked Greg.

"Well, the capture plan has to have a plan B. If James gets away from me, it sure would be nice to have Henry there to meet him at the gate in Taipei. They don't have the universal public camera coverage like we have here," answered Reece.

"Henry Swenson has yet to land in Alaska. How about sending him back to Taipei to be there in the event that James Wang gets ahead of you?" asked Greg.

"What about the perpetrator we have in custody? We can't just leave him on the tarmac somewhere," noted Reece.

"Have our new friend, John Collie, the Air Marshal, continue to Washington with him," answered Greg.

"Good idea, Greg. But I'm going to let you contact Henry with YOUR brilliant idea," replied Reece.

"How is he going to get from Elmendorf to Taipei? Who is going to take custody of Fred?" asked Greg.

"As you told me, General Broadtail is now working with us. It's time to find out if he really is. He agreed to the flight from Kadena and the stopover at Elmendorf. With the VP assassination, the ante has increased," answered Reece. "Call him to see if you can get him to help on this."

"Will do. There is shutdown of all flights out of the country. The question is, how does James think he is going to do that? Drive to Canada and catch a flight there? All the more reason to make sure Henry is there to greet him if he does get away," said Greg as he hung up.

Farragut Square and The Pentagon
10:00 am East Coast time

The beautiful Farragut Square Park, which is one of many in the downtown DC area, was now a war zone. It was only one block by one block, but now was the center of all law enforcement in the Washington area. The vice president, Emily Spring, had been assassinated. She never had a chance. It was a direct hit.

"How did they know which car she was in?" questioned the Secret Service officer who appeared to be in charge.

"Luck?" was the reply he got from his fellow agent.

"Here is the launch tube. It has a product and serial number on it. Contact the Pentagon to tell them we have something of theirs," said the first agent.

The agent immediately called the office to get the number for the Pentagon. After getting the number, he proceeded to call.

"Hello, this is the Secret Service. It appears we have a part from one of your weapon here in Farragut Square. It was used to kill the vice president," he told the person on the phone.

"What? The vice president is dead?" she asked.

"Yes, ma'am. Now who do I have to talk to about missing weapons?" the agent continued.

"Let me connect you to the communications office," she replied.

"Pentagon communications," was the next person on the line.

After explaining a disbelieving officer, probably a major or a colonel, he was directed to three more people until finally to the office of Major General Binder.

"This is General Binder. You have something of mine?" he asked.

"Yes, sir, I believe so. I'm with the Secret Service. I'm at Farragut Square with a launch tube with the product ID and serial number I gave your assistant. It was used to assassinate the vice president," responded the agent.

"Oh, boy, that's terrible. When did this happen? There is nothing on the news about this," asked General Binder.

"I know, sir. It happened about 15 minutes ago. We are still trying to determine what happened. Can you get someone down here so we can confirm this is yours?" clarified the agent.

"Absolutely. I'll have someone there as fast as they can get through traffic," answered General Binder.

The general called one of his colonels in and instructed him to get to Farragut Square, ASAP.

His next call was to his superior, General Rest.

"General, I believe we have found the missing personal bunker buster," stated General Binder.

"Good soldier," responded General Rest.

"No, sir, it's not good. The new weapon was used to assassinate the vice president," explained General Binder.

"Are you sure about it being our weapon and that the vice president was assassinated?" asked General Rest.

"Not sure about the weapon yet. I have sent Colonel Legion to determine that. The Secret Service has confirmed to me that Vice President Emily Spring was in the vehicle and was killed," responded General Binder.

"Oh my God. Who was behind this, and why?" said General Rest.

"They don't know yet," responded General Binder.

Washington, DC
10:15 a.m.

The White House was in chaos. Vice President Emily Spring had been assassinated. President Sessions was in the Oval Office with several of his top advisors. They were to meet with the full National Security Council in the Situation Room in about 15 minutes.

"How did this happen?" President Sessions asked Harriet Venti, the Director of Homeland Security.

"A stolen new weapon called the personal bunker buster was used," answered Harriet.

"What, our weapon? How did the people get it? Is it an act of terrorism?" demanded a now shouting President Sessions.

"Sir," interrupted his chief of staff, Roger Edwards, "The news media has it already. They have divulged that Vice President Spring was in the destroyed SUV."

"So much for instant information in today's world," responded President Sessions.

They all headed down to the Situation Room. The room was filling up with people from the Pentagon, the National Security Staff, and several members of the Cabinet.

It was apparent that there was no information from the NSA or any of the intelligence agencies regarding this attack. There had not been any chatter on any communication media that were being monitored.

Daniel Broadtail, the four-star general who was the Joint Chief of Staff, took the floor. "Gentlemen and ladies, I hate to inform you, but the weapon used to assassinate Vice President Spring was one of our newest and most effective weapons. It was stolen from the Aberdeen Proving Grounds earlier this week. We became aware of it missing and were in the middle of that investigation when this occurred. The launch tube was found at the scene at Farragut Square. The perpetrators knew what to steal. This one was the D model. The A model was to penetrate and apprehend. This model was a modified flash bang, no damage, no one hurt, but stunned. The B model was to penetrate and blast with an electromagnetic pulse to not kill people but to destroy all electronics. The C model was to penetrate and capture all intelligence. It left electronics in place but injured people. The D was to penetrate and destroy everything."

"If we don't know who is behind this then we have to shut down our borders and not let the perpetrators out of the country. Do it now!" emphatically stated President Sessions.

"Yes, sir," responded Harriet Venti, the Director of Homeland Security.

She immediately called her office to implement this command. This was not going to be pretty. It was on the scale of what the country did during the post September 11, 2001, World Trade Tower attack. The chaos of stopping all international flights and grounding those in flight was a big deal. But so was the assassination of the vice president. The news media was going to love this.

New York City

"This is Fox News with a Fox News Alert. The vice president, Emily Spring, has been assassinated in Washington, DC, today at about 10:15 a.m. We have been informed that a new military weapon that had been stolen from Aberdeen Proving Grounds was used to kill her. This weapon is called the Personal Bunker Buster. The PBB was developed for our special services to eliminate all persons in a building without actually entering. The weapon penetrates the outer walls and then detonates a high capacity bomb that has been delivered into the building. The government is informing us that there will be an air travel restriction. We now take you to our correspondent, Kelly Wright, in Washington. Kelly . . ."

"I'm in the White House briefing room. The president's press secretary is to come out and brief us any moment now. What you reported is all we know right now. It's now starting," Kelly Wright responded.

The White House press secretary spoke. "I'm sorry to report to the nation that our vice president, Emily Spring, was assassinated at 10:15 this morning. She had just left the White House grounds on her way back to the vice president's residence at the US Naval Observatory. A new weapon that was stolen earlier this week from Aberdeen Proving Grounds hit her vehicle. We don't have any information regarding the person or persons behind such a terrible attack on the United States of America. In response, the president has directed that all international air traffic be halted to prevent the perpetrator from leaving US soil. We did this previously after the attack on the World Trade Center on 9/11. When we identify the perpetrators, we'll permit flights to resume. We recognize the pain this inflicts upon all Americans but we need to trap the people behind this atrocity."

The room was filled with several reporters yelling questions. The press secretary waved everyone off saying that they did not have any additional information.

"This is Kelly Wright, you heard it. A tragedy, and our government does not know anything."

"Thank you, Kelly. We'll be back on this News Alert when we know more." The Fox News interruption team signed off.

It was going to be a difficult situation for the new media. They had the crime of the century and no information to give to the public that was desperate to know more.

On the way to Short Hills, New Jersey
About 1:00 p.m.

On the drive to New Jersey, Reece had tuned in to the radio. He was getting the tragic news about the assassination of Emily Spring over and over. Reece was certain that James Wang was behind this event. *"That was the explosion I heard. Wow, this is getting more complicated,"* thought Reece.

"Greg, this is Reece. I heard on the radio about the assassination of the vice president. I do believe James Wang was responsible for that dastardly deed. I saw him leave the White House quickly and go down into the subway. As I entered the subway, I heard the explosion that killed the VP. I don't believe in coincidences. He had to be behind this. I cannot understand why. I'll contact FBI Director Smith with this information."

"Do that. Jeff is at the FBI headquarters interrogating Peter Huang at this moment," answered Greg.

"Any status on James?" asked Reece.

"Traffic cams indicate that he is at home on the Ellis compound. I have not been able to hack the Ellis security system yet. When I do, I'll call you," answered Greg.

Reece called the private line for Director Smith.

"Hello, Reece. The ante has been raised down here," said Smitty, answering Reece's call.

"Yes, sir. I heard on the radio. I do believe my target, James Wang, is behind the assassination," stated Reece.

"What makes you think that, Reece?" asked Director Smith.

"I was watching him first at Farragut Square and then in Lafayette Park. He then went over and was talking with a uniformed

Secret Service person at the gate. As the SUVs came out, James Wang immediately called someone, and at a very fast pace went to the McPherson Square Metro Station. I lost him there. But we have him under surveillance right now."

"What did he do to make the assassination possible?" queried Smitty.

"Sir, I think someone directing the SUVs thought about which car the vice president was in. James Wang was able to intercept that information with the hearing device. He then relayed that information to the shooter at Farragut Square. The shooter knew with certainly which SUV had the vice president in it," explained Reece.

"Reece, what was the purpose of this?" asked Director Smith.

"I think it was the proof of theft signal to their clients. I don't think these guys who work for the Ministry of State Security are the people behind this. They are just being capitalists, as are any Chinese organization. They want to benefit from our capitalist economic model like everyone else. They have a client who is paying for the devices. The two guys we have captured were testing the devices, and their individual rewards were the bonuses they made gambling. Peter Huang sent the money to his personal Cayman Island account. That's now his money, as far as he was concerned," explained Reece.

"What about your guy in New Jersey?" asked Director Smith.

"I don't know. His task was to set up the theft of the PBB from the Aberdeen Proving grounds and then the assassination. He is back home as if nothing has happened. I can't make the move on him yet for two reasons. One, he is at Oliver Ellis' compound, which is a fortress, and two, upon what basis do I confront him?"

"We have Peter Huang in interrogation right now. I'll let Jeff know your theory. I'll also contact Henry. He is in flight bringing Fred Tsim back here. Perhaps Henry should wake him up and ask him a few questions using the device," said Smitty.

"Not sure Henry should wake the guy up. He is too dangerous. I'll keep you posted when James makes a move again. I have arranged for Henry to fly back to Taipei to greet James in the event he escapes. Greg should be breaking the news to Henry when he lands in Elmendorf this afternoon," Reece said as he hung up.

Reece realized that he'd left Tori on Monday in a cloud of confusion. He thought, *"This is no way to treat the woman you love. She is probably really upset with me and worried at the same time. Time to do something about that."*

"Hello, Reece. I was wondering when you would surface. Are you OK?" answered Tori.

"Yes, I'm sorry. I was working with the guys non-stop. Since this is not a secure connection, let me explain in general terms," answered Reece. "Yes, I know about the vice president. I was nearby, but not close enough to be in danger. I know who did it and I'm in pursuit. We have caught two of the three perpetrators. It's a bit interesting because the third one does not seem to be concerned about his being identified or caught. I'll have Greg contact you with updates a little more frequently. I love you, and cannot wait for all of this to be over."

"I love you too. Please be careful. Apparently these are dangerous people," commented Tori.

"Yes they are and I'll be very careful. Bye for now," said Reece as he hung up slowly as he envisioned a soft kiss to lower his anxiety.

Reece was more concerned than what he communicated to Tori. His target was dangerous. He did not seem to be concerned about getting out of the country or being found. *"What does he know that I don't know?"* thought Reece.

"Reece, this is Greg. I talked with General Broadtail. He is on board to get Henry back to Taiwan. He is also sending a couple MPs to help John Collie escort the perpetrator to Washington. I'm still working with General Broadtail on a contingency plan on how to beam you to Taiwan if that has to happen," said Greg.

"Good going. I'm almost to the Ellis compound. Any ideas?"

Short Hills, New Jersey
2:00 p.m. East Coast time

James was relieved that he was able to leave the Washington, DC, area without interruption. He did listen to the radio on the drive home. The government was in a panic. They announced that all international commercial flights were being cancelled. The country was on a shutdown. They were now trying to trap him here. But he had other plans.

He pulled into the garage and went into the mansion. Mr. Ellis was in his office on the phone and did not hear James come into the residence. James could hear the conversation through the french doors to the loggia located just outside the office. The curtains were drawn, which meant that Mr. Ellis was going to open the safe. James expected that. The trip tomorrow was scheduled, and he was going to bring at least one bag of diamonds.

"Yes, Harry, I'll be there on time, despite what my government is doing. We have a deal and I intend to make the acquisition. Are all the principals set up for our meeting? Good, then I'll see you this weekend. Yes, I do have my reservations at The Riviera Hotel. See you there for the breakfast buffet. I'm looking forward to that. It's the best in Taipei." Then Oliver Ellis hung up.

James could hear through the french doors that the Behrens painting was being moved and the safe was now exposed.

Oliver thought as he retrieved the diamonds required for this trip, "*I do believe that two bags are necessary to make this deal. Diamonds have been appreciating again. Over the past few years they did take a dive, but no one doubts the future value. Put a bag of diamonds to be valued at one hundred million dollars down on the table and anyone will drool. Two bags and they will normally flip. This is a flip deal. Two hundred million as a down payment for a two billion dollar venture. OK, hand on the reader, remembering the alpha number sequence input that was 21 characters is almost impossible for even me to comprehend. Good thing it's a phrase to me. 2B@TheRightPlaceIsGr8t!. Oh, what a beautiful sight. I should put these two bags into my case. I know it's only James and me, but we do have to drive to the airport tomorrow. This combination is easier, zero, five, four, four, seven. Now lock it, dummy. You still have eight bags to protect."*

James now knew the combination to both the safe and the carrying case. That's what he needed. The presence on the loggia would be normal for him this time of the day. Mr. Ellis liked a glass of wine there about this time. James set about putting his glass of 2004 Carneros della Notte D III Vineyard Pinot

Noir on the side table to his favorite outdoor chair. It was one of Mr. Ellis' favorites. He had visited the vineyard in Carneros, California, and bought a few cases for his wine cellar. James never acquired the taste for wine, but Mr. Ellis more than had that acquired taste for the two of them.

"It would be a mistake to put anything into Mr. Ellis' wine. He would probably tell by the bouquet that something was not right. He always took great pleasure in checking the bouquet, then the visual clarity, and finally a sip. I'll miss those performances."

James then also put out some cheese and crackers that complemented the wine. Mr. Ellis so enjoyed the ritual of having fine wine, a paired "snack," as he called it, and reading on his iPad. Just as James had set up everything, Oliver Ellis came through the french doors of his office onto the loggia.

"Ah, James, you spoil me. You know exactly what I both need and want. Is it CDN?" exclaimed Oliver. Oliver's nickname for Carneros della Notte was CDN.

"But of course, sir. I knew you were in a celebratory mood and wanted your favorite," responded James. "Do you want music, sir?"

"Yes, put on the Enya set," replied Oliver. Although Enya had not recorded in many years, she was one of Mr. Ellis' favorite performers. He found her music both soothing and exciting at the same time.

Soon the air was filled with music, the sound of "ahs" for the wine enjoyment, and water sounding in the nearby fountain. Oliver thoroughly enjoyed his house. He had an architect in Skaneateles, New York, design the house based upon one the architect had designed a number of years ago. It had plenty of room, and was laid out for both entertaining and personal enjoyment. It had a fully functioning office complex on one end of the house. He used it for some strategic meetings. His personal office was off the library and isolated. The loggia was off the great room and his office. This was where he spent most of his time.

James had work to do very soon. He had to prepare for the trip tomorrow and the early morning events that resulted in HIS bonus. His was more because of his imbedded assignment and the extra task in Washington today. James would retire on his bonus to somewhere in the warmer part of the world. He still had not made up his mind where yet.

After an hour, James felt he could interrupt Mr. Ellis' enjoyable time on the loggia.

"Sir, are you aware of the events that occurred in Washington today?" inquired James.

"Yes, such a tragedy. What a shock for us all," answered Oliver.

"Will the flight restrictions prevent us from our travel plans tomorrow, sir?" inquired James.

"No, it won't. I called earlier today and got special clearance for us to leave. It's not like they would suspect either you or me for such a dastardly deed. Right, James?" replied Oliver.

"Of course not, sir," said James, almost not containing what he was really thinking.

"Of course not! Wow, if only he or anyone else knew who was behind this or what was at stake."

Elmendorf Air Force Base, Alaska
11:30 p.m. AKDT; 3:30 p.m. EDT

The flight from Okinawa was without incident.

Henry introduced himself to the base commander. The commander, a lieutenant general, was curious regarding this irregular mission. Henry informed him that this was part of a program that was classified POTUS eyes only. The general knew that this situation was above even his pay grade. The military fully understands the chain of command. Lieutenant General Steven "Buzz" Jeer was already ahead of Henry.

Buzz had received a call from General Broadtail, the Chairman of the Joint Chiefs of Staff. As high up the command as Buzz wanted to hear from. Buzz was told to expect Henry with his "cargo" in tow. He was instructed to have Henry contact Greg Mays when he arrived.

They walked into Buzz's office. Henry called Greg.

"Hi, Greg. What's up?" Henry said, answering Greg's greeting.

"Well, Henry, lots happening here. The critical thing is that VP Spring was assassinated earlier today. We think the perpetrator you have and the one still on the loose are behind that event," said Greg.

"Wow, that's major league! What's the plan?" commented Henry.

"The third guy has eluded us once already. We have a lockdown on flights out of the country. That should stop him, but Reece feels we should have a backup plan in the event this guy has an alternate plan to get out of the country. We think he is headed to Taipei. That's based on the fact that the other two perpetrators were headed there. Here's the plan: General Jeer will get you to Taipei. Air Marshal John Collie will escort your perpetrator to DC. General Jeer will send two MPs to assist John," said Greg.

"OK, I should have known I was going to have more fun," lamented Henry.

New York's JFK

This is probably the only airport that understood the shutdown of all international flights. Not that it made it fun to be there. It's the fifth-busiest airport in the United States. There are over 70,000 passengers using it every day. Atlanta is almost twice that volume. The international flights were stopped for obvious reasons. The intent was to prevent whoever was responsible for the death of Vice President Emily Spring from leaving US soil.

The news was as would be expected. It was on the scale of the September 11 World Trade Center attack and JFK assassination of 1963 all rolled up into one. Not only were the planes not flying but the airports were at a heightened level of alert. People, taxies, buses, personal cars, airport personnel, and security staff were in a cornucopia of confusion. The question was how long was this going to last? The news media could not get an answer from the government. This country depends on flying people all over the world for both business and pleasure. For the past 10 years, air travel had grown an average of 5 percent per year, even considering the big downturn in 2009.

Los Angeles' airport, LAX, was not much better. All of the international hubs had significantly inconvenienced travelers. Meetings at far-off locations that would be missed. Funerals and weddings that would occur without everyone there, including sometimes the bride or the groom. It was a significant event. People were going to remember this for many years.

The phones were ringing off the hook at the airlines, the various government alphabet entities, TSA, FAA, FBI, and others. No answers were available at any of them. The country was in a lockdown, with no one with enough knowledge to permit flights.

CHAPTER EIGHT

Friday

Short Hills, New Jersey

Oliver Ellis was an early riser. He had a long day today for the flight to Taipei. His Gulfstream 650ER was the model that had a range of 7,500 nautical miles to make this flight over the polar cap to Taipei without refueling. The plane had a private cabin in the aft portion of the plane so he could work, sleep, eat, or have a confidential meeting. Oliver was raised on a farm, then moved to London in the financial sector. Early mornings were standard, and so was hard work. His upbringing stood him in good stead. He went down to the kitchen and saw that James had already prepared a breakfast for him. The coffee smelled especially good. He sat at the alcove table and first had a sip of the V-8 juice. It was his favorite morning drink to start the day. Oliver opened up the *Wall Street Journal* application on his iPad, as was his usual habit.

"Oh, how could I live without James? He anticipates my every need and makes it seamless for me," thought Oliver.

Little did Oliver know, but soon he would experience a side of James he never expected.

James came into the kitchen and asked if there was anything special Mr. Ellis wanted him to do in preparation for the flight.

"Just get my suitcase from my bedroom and bring it to the car. I'll get my briefcase from my office in a minute and we can go," replied Ellis.

James left and waited in the hallway for the flunitrazepam to take effect. The strong flavor of V-8 was great for hiding the flunitrazepam James had added. Flunitrazepam is an illegal drug in the US. James obtained it in China and had it shipped to him via diplomatic pouch by a friend. It's also known as the date rape drug "roofie." Soon Ellis would lose his ability to stand or talk.

It was taking longer than James thought. He then went upstairs to get the suitcase that was not going to leave the house today. As he came down he yelled out to Mr. Ellis, "Sir, I have your bag. Do you have the briefcase?"

There was no reply. The drug must have kicked in. As James entered the kitchen, he saw Mr. Ellis slumped over in his chair in what appeared to be a daze. *"Perfect,"* thought James. He needed Mr. Ellis to be alive, but not in control of his faculties.

The safe in the office contained another eight bags of diamonds. No one else knew that Oliver Ellis had an inventory of some $1 billion of diamonds. He had taken $200 million out of the safe last night. It did not occur to James that he was being greedy to get the remaining eight bags.

The safe had two biometric requirements that were unique. Not only did you have to know the alphanumeric combination, you had to put your eye to the retina scanner and your right hand on the hand reader. The hand reader would only accept Mr. Ellis' live hand. It was not just the image of his finger/palm print, but the sensor had to detect blood flow and a pulse in the hand. The flunitrazepam did not affect the hand. However, too much, and Ellis would not be able to keep his eyelids open. James was careful not to exceed the amount that would kill him. That was six drops. If he did that, his heart would stop in three minutes. His dose was to be 2 to 3 drops. He used two to be certain that he did not kill him.

James lifted Oliver out of the chair and carried him to his office. He pulled aside the Behrens painting, exposing the safe. He then input the alphanumeric combination he got from Mr. Ellis' thinking the night before, 2B@TheRightPlaceIsGr8t!. James raised Oliver's head so the eye scanner would function on his right eye. It was open and in position. The scanner turned the monitoring LED to green, thereby indicating that it was successful. James then positioned Oliver's right hand on the hander reader. The hand rested on the structure with its own weight. The reader also changed the system indicator to a green LED illumination, thereby indicating a successful read.

James now longer needed Oliver's body or mind. However, he had to make sure that it did not fall. The system had a sound override in the event that someone invaded at this point. James put Oliver down in his chair carefully. Then James opened the safe. There, neatly piled in the safe, were the remaining eight bags of diamonds. Carefully, James removed them and put them on top of the desk. James then closed the safe and put the Behrens painting back in place.

It was time to get out of the compound and to the airport.

James left Oliver slumped over in his chair. Although he was tempted to finish the job and end Oliver's life, he felt some personal connection to the man he had served for over five years. *"Yes, $200 million a year is not a bad compensation package for those five years,"* he thought.

He grabbed the briefcase with the first two bags and his new pile of eight bags that was in the duffle bag he had left in the office earlier that morning. He went straight to the car parked out front and headed to the airport. It was better that Mr. Ellis used the Morristown Municipal Airport, located about five miles away. The Newark airport was about the same distance away but the security would be less friendly. Mr. Ellis had his own hangar at the airport. Because of that, he could drive into the hangar and "get Mr. Ellis aboard" without anyone actually seeing him.

Reece was located down the road from the Ellis compound. He watched James drive the car past but without anyone else in the car. He was not driving above the speed limit. *"He is one cool character,"* thought Reece. Reece called Greg to update him. He had asked Greg to hack into the Ellis security system yesterday. So far, no news back.

"Hi, Greg. My target is on the move," said Reece.

"I know," said Greg. "I was just able to hack into the Ellis system about 15 minutes ago. Oliver Ellis is in his office, sitting in his chair. It does not look good. He appears to be slumped over," continued Greg.

"Is there blood around?" asked Reece.

"No, he just looks like he fell asleep. I can see his chest move while breathing," answered

Greg. "I saw James take a suitcase, briefcase, and a duffle bag to the car."

"I'm driving behind James. He is my target. Oliver Ellis will have to wait," said Reece.

Morristown Municipal Airport

James was well-known at the airport. There was no problem driving onto the premises and straight into the Ellis hangar. Within the hangar was Oliver's Gulfstream 650ER jet. It was ready for the flight to Taipei, Taiwan. The crew of three was moving around doing pre-flight checks.

James went up the stairs with the suitcase and duffle bag. He saw the pilot and asked if they had put extra provisions on board for this flight. James had hired Matthew some four years ago.

"Hello, Mr. Wang," said Matthew.

"Oh, hello, Matthew. Sorry I'm so abrupt. Mr. Ellis is so focused regarding this trip," answered James.

James then said, "I thought I saw a tire on the starboard side a little soft. Would you check it for me?"

Matthew got up and went down the stairs to examine it. James went with him. They examined the tires and got out a gauge to make sure.

A few minutes later, they returned to the plane. James went back to the private compartment for Mr. Ellis. The configuration of this plane provided a private portion of the plane so Oliver Ellis could relax, sleep, eat, and think without interruption. Only James was allowed to enter. The crew was aware of Oliver Ellis' idiosyncrasies.

James returned to the cockpit and said, "Mr. Ellis is settled and wanted to know how long until we depart."

Matthew responded, "I have a few more system checks to do with Chris. In about five minutes. I did not see Mr. Ellis come aboard." Matthew was referring to Chris Cell, the copilot.

"I saw him go up the stairs while we were getting the tire gauge. You know how he is on this long flight. He gets into his zone to work, sleep, and eat while you get us there," replied James.

The flight plan called for an international flight. Commercial flights check your passport when you enter. That's because you need the passport to come back to the United States. You don't present the passport to a government official to leave the country; outbound travelers have to show a passport only on commercial airlines. Therefore, Mr. Ellis was on the plane and part of the manifest because James said so. The crew would not know that Mr. Ellis was not on board if James handled it properly. He had always made it a routine to keep Mr. Ellis remote to the crew, so this was not unusual.

After 10 minutes, Matthew went on the speaker system and told James the flight was ready to roll.

As they taxied to the runway, James started to fear that Mr. Ellis' pull was not enough to permit his escape from the US. After all, everyone else was in the international flight shutdown. In ten minutes James took a deep breath in as they lifted off and were taking their heading of 345° with a distance of some 6,777 nautical miles to Taipei (TPE). It should take about 12 hours with the plane flying at 0.85 Mach. The speed is about 652 miles per hours. Most commercial aircraft flights fly much slower to save on fuel. The G650ER can fly at 0.90 Mach, but that would cut the range. It was more important to leave the country NOW and get to Taiwan without any interruptions. The flight path over the polar route is not how commercial aircraft fly, but the Gulfstream G650ER has the avionics that permit such a direct route.

James was smiling with the knowledge that he was soon to be enjoying the fruits of Mr. Ellis' lifelong work. His aircraft had a sticker price of something above $66.5 million. This was slightly more because of his custom interior. *"Thank you, Oliver, for taking care of me. Oh, and thank you for my retirement nest egg,"* thought James.

James had put the duffle bag and the briefcase in the private quarters. It was safe there. No one would dare enter without checking with James first.

The flight attendant, Lisa Carter, came to James while he sat in his usual chair just outside the private quarters.

"Can I get you anything, James?" asked Lisa. She called James by his first name. He had hired her and she was immensely grateful. The job was really a cushy one. She worked only when Mr. Ellis was flying. However, she was paid as if she was working 24/7. With the airline, the pay was when the plane's door closed and until it opened. She really liked this gig. Mr. Ellis was courteous but did not try to be close friends. He was Mr. Ellis to her. It was his plane, she was part of the crew, paid very well, and had job security. The only drawback was she was to be available 24/7. When Mr. Ellis wanted to go somewhere, she was to be there. That was the same for the other crewmembers. No one complained; no one in the industry was compensated as well as they were.

"Yes, can I have a Bloody Mary, Lisa?" answered James. He felt like celebrating.

"Does Mr. Ellis want anything?" Lisa asked, to be careful to respect Mr. Ellis' privacy.

"No, he told me that he wanted to be by himself for most of this flight. I'll let you know when he wants something to drink or eat," responded James. "This is one of his biggest deals this year and he needs to get his mind into the game, as he says."

Lisa smiled, and knew that this was not unusual. When Mr. Ellis was on the hunt for a new acquisition he was focused, and nothing else got into his head. It was James' and Lisa's job to protect the boss.

She went to the galley and got a Bloody Mary for James.

"Here you are. Ring me if you want anything else," said Lisa with a sincere smile.

"Thank you, Lisa," replied James.

Short Hills, New Jersey

Reece followed Oliver Ellis' car to the Morristown Municipal Airport. He watched as the car approached and went into the Ellis hangar. It was impossible to see what was happening, since he had to pass through a security checkpoint to enter the property and he was not going to get close enough to find out. His only option was to watch from outside the perimeter. After about 25 minutes, Reece saw the Ellis G650ER with is an E-O logo leaving the hangar. The E within the O was very distinctive. It was like Trump on his 757. It announced that the "man" had arrived. Ellis was not the type of person to be ostentatious, but he had to create the aura so his deals would be unquestioned. He was not one to be turned down or played with. His persona was actually folksier, but the outside world saw him as a forceful, powerful billionaire.

As Reece watched the plane leave the hangar he thought, *"How is this guy leaving the country? There is a shutdown of all international flights."*

Reece called Greg and told him about the plane coming out of the hangar and taxiing down to the runway.

"How is this guy permitted to fly with a ban on international flights?" Reece asked Greg.

"Let me check to see if there is a flight plan registered," replied Greg.

"Reece, we are seeing the power of a billionaire in action. The flight plan is to fly from Morristown Municipal Airport to the Taoyuan International Airport," Greg continued after a few computer clicks.

"Greg, Oliver Ellis is not on that plane. You saw him in his office. I saw James alone in the car!" exclaimed Reece. "With that plane, James will be in Taiwan in 12 hours. I need to have the Star Trek team beam me over there to catch up. I cannot let him get away!"

"What do you want me to do?" asked Greg.

"See if we can get me to Taiwan as fast as I can. Once he is there, he will be almost impossible to find!" screamed Reece. It was rare that Reece was overtly emotional but he was now really afraid of losing this guy. His normal 40s heart rate must have been close to 120 bpm.

Calming down, Reece then said, "Thank God you thought ahead and had Henry return to Taiwan."

"Ok, I'll work on getting you there ASAP," replied Greg in a very calm voice, trying to bring Reece down a notch or two. Greg could only remember once when Reece was this close to exploding. It was a mission to Iraq where they had to take out a tribal leader that was supporting ISIS. They lost that guy too. But that was in the hot desert, with no one friendly to work with. That event taught them about CIA spy satellites and the detail that was available.

"Greg, I want to get Agent Sarah Castle there with me. If we show up as a British couple, the perpetrator will less suspicious that we are there for him. Include that in your planning," replied Reece.

"I'll call General Broadtail for help on that. He must be on a first-name basis with William Shatner, aka Captain Kirk," said Greg with a sly smile on his face.

Greg was also trying to work up a plan on how to find this guy in Taiwan with a two-hour head start. Time to call the boss, Bruce Hardy. He may know more on tracking than either Greg or Reece. This guy is so good that Henry may not be able to keep track of him when he arrives.

"Reece, before you go ballistic, how about going back to the Ellis compound and see if you can get any information from Oliver Ellis. He does not seem to be dead, only drugged-out," continued Greg.

"Good idea, Greg. I'm glad someone is calm around here," replied Reece.

Reece headed back to the Ellis compound. In about seven minutes, Reece was at the front gate. As he approached, the gates opened. Greg must have not only cracked the video system at the Ellis compound but the security control system as well. Reece mouthed a "Thank you" to the video monitor as he went through. He was certain Greg was watching on the other end.

Reece ran up the stairs of the entryway and turned the knob. Once again, he had an unchallenged entry. *"Oh, Greg, you're slick,"* thought Reece. Reece had no idea where the office was located. Greg, sensing that, called Reece.

"Reece, I thought a little help on navigation was needed," said Greg when Reece answered the phone.

"You betcha, it would help."

"Go into the foyer and turn left into the music room. Directly across the room is a door that goes into a library. As you enter the library, on the right is a door that leads into Oliver Ellis' office. You will see him slumped in his chair behind the desk, which is at the far end of the office."

As Reece entered, he could not help but whistle at the beauty of Oliver Ellis' house. It was befitting a billionaire. He went through the foyer, through the music room, through the library, and into the office. There, as described by Greg, was Oliver Ellis, slumped over his desk.

"Hello, Mr. Ellis. Are you able to talk?" asked Reece.

Reece realized that Oliver Ellis was in need of medical help but he was not in a position to render aid.

"Greg, he is still out of it. He needs medical attention. Please contact the local 9-1-1 people. I'm going to get out of here before they come so I'm not caught up in this situation," said Reece.

"Will do. I have to get a plan for you to be beamed to Taiwan. I have a call in to Captain Kirk and the *Enterprise*," replied Greg, referring to Star Trek elements.

"On Mr. Ellis' desk is a notation about Oliver Ellis staying at the Riviera Hotel in Taipei. If I was a betting man, I'm betting that's where James is headed. He needs to keep the deception alive as long as he can," said Reece.

Washington, DC

Greg's house office (loaded with computers and electronic gear)

After Greg got off the phone with Reece, he thought about how he could "beam" Reece to Taiwan. They were sure that James Wang was headed there. The other two perpetrators had been on their way to Taiwan. It made sense for all of them to gather there first.

It was now about 10:15 a.m.

Greg called General Broadtail to discuss options.

After a couple hours, Greg called Reece.

"Reece, I have a plan that will work with help from General Broadtail. This is his idea, and it's going to require some coordination," stated Greg.

"OK, spill the beans."

"If I remember correctly, you're SR-71 qualified. Right?" continued Greg.

"Yes, it was a couple years ago and it's not fun to fly that baby. I also want to take Agent Sarah Castle with me as part of my cover when I'm in Taiwan," Reece answered with hesitation.

"I know, the Blackbird has two seats," answered Greg with a hint of humor. He knew it had two seats, neither of which was as comfortable as the Ryan Air economy seats.

"Well, you know the official position of the government is that all the SR-71 planes are either on display or were lost. As we both know there is one in Okinawa, one in McGuire Air Force Base in New Jersey, and the third is shared between Thule Air Base in Greenland and Ali Al Salem Air Base in Kuwait," continued Greg.

"You're not far from McGuire. Agent Castle will meet you at McGuire," Greg explained.

"Oh my, this sounds like a plan that's going to be interesting. Remember, the SR-71 only has a range of 3,200 miles, and it's almost 7,800 miles from New Jersey to Taipei," commented Reece, not liking this solution. He knew about the small seating and the flight suits required to fly a plane that flew at Mach 3.2. That's 3.2 times the speed of sound.

"OK, here's the complete story. You take off from New Jersey, fly over the Atlantic for your top-off refueling and then head to Alaska. The distance to the US/Canadian border is about 3,100 miles. That will take you about one hour and 15 minutes. A KC-135 will meet you there to refuel. You will have to drop in altitude and slow down to 530 mph. You will go back up to altitude and speed to fly to the other end of Alaska, to an area near Attu Island. It's about 1,300 miles west of Anchorage. Another KC-135 will meet you there to top off the tanks again. That will give you enough fuel to fly the rest of the way to Okinawa. You land there, and the fly boys will take you to Taipei in style," said Greg with a slight smirk.

The silence on Reece's end was deafening.

Greg was proud of his planning. "Hello, Reece. You still there?" asked Greg, knowing that Reece was really not a fan of the plan, but Star Trek beaming equipment was still not available.

"Oh, with this plan, I believe you'll be in Taipei about three hours before James Wang. That's based on his flying Mr. Ellis' G650ER, which has a range of 8,631 miles flying at Mach 0.85, ok, at 652 mph. Your speed, at 2,455 mph, does make up time," said Greg, now with a big smile on his face.

"Are you sure we can pull this off?" asked Reece, not really excited about the flight plan.

"Yes, I already checked with General Broadtail. He has the equipment and personnel in place for you. Agent Castle is on her way to New Jersey as we speak," Greg replied with another grin. "You just need to get to McGuire as fast as you can. Your flight leaves at noon."

"Ok, not really an option, but it does deliver," said Reece with a sigh of resignation.

"Hey, no TSA hassle for you!" said Greg, trying to add humor. "I have a few presents for you to take to help with surveillance in Asia. I have a friend who knew someone who worked on the sophisticated animal robots for the PBS show *Spy in the Wild*. You will love them. I can control them from here and support you. Now, get booking."

In the G650ER

James Wang finally settled in for the little over ten-hour flight to Taipei. He had no trouble leaving US airspace due to Oliver Ellis' pull. He just needed to satisfy the crew that Mr. Ellis was in the back of the plane in his quarters and wanted to be left alone.

The flight attendant, Lisa Carter, was hired by James, and knew that she had this cushy job due to James. Normally Mr. Ellis did not interface with the flight deck crew. That was fortunate on this flight, since Mr. Ellis was not on board.

"Lisa, can I have another Bloody Mary? Make it a double," James asked Lisa.

"Sure, Mr. Wang. Is there anything I need to get Mr. Ellis?" answered Lisa.

"No, he said he wanted to rest on this flight. I made a big breakfast for him this morning and gave him a lunch to go for the flight. I would be surprised if he came out of his quarters at all," answered James.

"Sure, one double Bloody Mary, coming up," Lisa said cheerfully.

"I wish I knew where Peter and Fred are now. We should have had a plan for if there was a problem. The radio silence was a nice idea for not having a cross connection to mission failure but does not consider errors. Oh well, in about two weeks I'll not have to think about any of this again. I'll be somewhere warm, with not a worry on my mind," thought James.

"Thank you, Lisa," said James as he took his double Bloody Mary.

The drone of the jet was very lulling. He felt as though it was in the morning that he should sleep. He would arrive in Taipei about eight thirty in the morning, but his body would still be at eight thirty in the evening. The only way to change his body clock was to sleep a few hours to permit him to start the day. He was to meet with Fred and Peter at The Riviera Hotel. It was Mr. Ellis' favorite place to stay.

The effects of the alcohol, relief that the hard part was now behind him, and the low frequency drone of the engines lulled James to sleep.

McGuire Air Force Base
New Jersey

McGuire Air Force Base and the Army's Fort Dix shared the site together. It was also home to many dedicated military personnel who protected the United States. In a hangar that was in an extra secure location was a large black airplane that was, according to official records, retired. However, this old bird, and two other ones like it, were in reality an ace up the sleeve for the military and CIA. This was an SR-71, the Blackbird. It flew at an altitude of 85,000 feet at a speed of 3.2 Mach. Commercial airliners fly up to 39,000 feet. The standard Boing 747s that fly around the world have a speed of 550 miles per hour, or 0.85 Mach. The Blackbird, at 3.2, would be going about 2,445 miles per hour. It was a technical marvel. No SR-71 planes had ever been shot down. It was reported that if a missile locked on for a kill shot, it would merely out-run the missile in speed and altitude. The current versions were upgraded with data links and new sensors. The other two locations were at the Kadena Air Force Base in Okinawa, Japan, and Thule Air Force Base in Greenland. The Blackbird at Thule was also based out of Ali Al Salem Air Base in Kuwait. All the bases were located with open water very adjacent so takeoffs and landings would not be easily noticed or monitored. Former astronaut and US Senator John Glenn would be proud that some minds realized what he knew about the strategic capability of this aircraft. Satellites have a lead-time to get to a location for reconnaissance. Satellites are also easily tracked, so the objects or people of interest can easily be moved or put under cover. The Blackbird was unpredictable and flexible. It could be anywhere it wanted to be without anyone knowing it was there. The new optical and sensor systems permitted it to detect through clouds, rain, dust, and most anything. It could even detect thermal images within buildings to find people.

As Reece approached the base entrance gate, he had a lump in his gut for this next phase. He was still not thrilled with the next few hours of cramped flying. He was unusual to be rated for flying the SR-71. Very few outside of the regular pilots were ever given the opportunity or went through the extensive qualifying rigors to be so qualified. President Ralph Winston thought it was a good idea, so it happened. How Greg knew about Reece's qualification was a mystery to him. He never mentioned it to the team while they were operating overseas.

"Sir, identification please," requested the guard at the entrance gate.

"Yes, sir. Here it is. My name is Reece Stanton," Reece answered respectfully.

The guard smartly saluted the civilian, an unusual action by military personnel to a civilian. However, it was a sign of ultimate respect, and Reece found out why in the next statement.

"Colonel Black is in the guard house waiting to escort you, sir!" responded the guard.

Reece knew Greg arranged this way up the ladder. Colonel Black was number 2 on this base. The only more significant situation would be for the base commander to escort him. Reece knew he would be meeting him soon.

"Colonel Black, this is Mr. Stanton, sir," introduced the guard.

"Leave your car here in the parking lot and jump in with me," said Colonel Black after shaking Reece's hand.

"Did my associate, Agent Sarah Castle, arrive yet?" Reece asked the colonel.

"Yes, she did. She got here about 30 minutes ago. We started to brief her on the mission," answered Colonel Black.

"Oh, I bet that was fun," quipped Reece, knowing that Sarah had no idea what a SR-71 was or what flying in one entailed.

"That, sir, is putting it mildly. When we fitted her for her flight suit and helmet she finally let out a scream of: **"Why did I ever get involved with Reece STANTON!"** It was so loud that the civilians off base must have heard her," answered the colonel, now with a slight smirk.

"Yeah, I told my coordinating team member to beam me to Taiwan, and this was the best he could do," replied Reece.

"Well, as you know, Mr. Stanton, flying the SR-71 is as close to beaming as we have without going into orbit," answered the colonel.

"Here we are," replied the colonel.

They had just entered a hangar at an isolated area of the base. There stood the Blackbird, and in a flight suit, one unhappy Agent Sarah Castle. She held her helmet and was talking to an airman who was explaining some finer point of being in the plane.

"Hi, Sarah It has been awhile since I saw you." said Reece in the friendliest voice he could muster, knowing he was about to get a fury of wrath from a very pretty, very smart, engineering CIA operative.

"Mr. Stanton, who came up with this harebrained idea?" was the first volley from Sarah.

Luckily it was not Reece's idea, and he slid that one off to Greg and Chairman of the Joint Chiefs of Staff Daniel Broadtail. "Sarah, not my idea. It was Greg and General Broadtail. They cooked this up. However, if it goes to plan, we'll be in Taipei three hours ahead of our perpetrator. We need to get to the hotel before him so he will not be suspicious. By the way, how is your British accent? That's our cover. I heard you could pull that off."

"My British accent will pass. I'm not sure my anger of being in such a small seat for hours is going to pass," quipped back Sarah.

"Fine, I'll have to live with that," replied Reece. "I have to get in my flight suit."

Reece was back after about 15 minutes, having found a flight suit and helmet that fit him. The SR-71 flies so fast that even at an altitude of 80,000 feet, the outside temperature would be close to -64°F, yet the skin of the plane's surface and the exterior of the windscreen could reach 600°F (316°C). The altitude created the need to wear pressurized suits and the helmets to supply sufficient oxygen to the occupants. It was not fun to fly in an SR-71. But it was an honor to fly one.

After about 30 minutes, the extra items from Greg and the small travel bags as part of the cover were loaded in the limited spaces in the plane. It was time for Reece and Sarah to get aboard. They did, and were wheeled out to the runway that took them out over the Atlantic.

The Blackbird would burn somewhat conventional JP-7 fuel, which was difficult to light. Consequently, it needed a startup of triethylborane (TEB) to burn first and get it all started. The green flame startled Sarah. She had not been told about this little sequence. Sensing this, Reece tried to calm Sarah and walk through this step and then the next few events.

"Sarah, relax. The fuel the SR-71 uses needs a booster that ignites upon exposure to air that creates a temperature that will then ignite the regular, stable JP-7 fuel. We are taking off over the Atlantic to avoid detection by anyone. Once we are a few miles out, a specialized refueling plane, a KC-135Q, will meet us and send out a refueling boom to connect just behind you on the fuselage. The guys doing this are good at what they do. Just enjoy them doing what they do so well. This whole thing is necessary because we cannot take off with a full tank. That's why we top off the tank once up in the air. Then we'll turn, go up to our altitude, and start the flight for about one hour and 16 minutes to the border between Alaska and Canada. There will be another KC-135Q there to greet us to refuel this hungry bird. Trust me, Sarah, there is another very skilled team in that second plane that will do exactly what the guys are going do for us in a few minutes," said Reece, trying to fill Sarah's technical brain with so many facts and thoughts that she was distracted from the new sounds and motions of a plane that wanted to go higher and faster than she had ever experienced—or for that matter, VERY few people had ever experienced.

"Thanks, Reece. What happens if they are not there on time?" said Sarah, always the doubting Thomas.

"Sarah, they will be there. This is what the military does, and does well. A mission, which is what we are on, is planned to the last detail. The guys and gals all know their respective roles and do their tasks to make the mission work. The US military is the best team in the world," answered Reece.

As they were just finishing the conversation, the KC-135Q was above them. Reece slowed the plane to the same speed and held the altitude steady. He just had to do that while the guys above and ahead of him did the rest. After what seemed like hours to Sarah, the fuel boom disengaged with a slight jolt.

Taking on her British persona, she yelled, "Bloody hell!"

"Relax, Sarah. We go faster without those guys attached," laughed Reece.

In a matter of moments, Reece guided the plane up to cruising altitude. He was going to stay at 80,000 feet for most of the flight.

"Now we take a heading of 320.24° and we'll get there in no time," Reece said as a matter of fact.

Sarah somehow managed to put an ear bud (only one, because she and Reece still needed to communicate) in one ear and held her iPod. She was content as she could be in the small cockpit area used by the reconnaissance systems officer to do his tasks. The hour and 15 minutes literally flew by to Sarah. She did observe to Reece a couple times, "It sure looks empty below. No cities, no roads, no sign of life."

"We just hit the northern parts of Canada. We started across Ontario, then Manitoba, Saskatchewan, Alberta, and British Columbia.

Those are provinces. We just left the southeast corner of the Northwest Territory and are currently over the Yukon Territory. The government setup is different for provinces and territories in Canada. Do you want me to continue?" answered Reece.

Sarah said, "Tell me more about yourself and the team you have put together. We do have time, do we not?"

Reece realized that Sarah has been thrown in with a bunch of guys who had worked together for years, and was actually on the outside looking in.

"Sure. I can talk about the other guys. You have talked with Greg Mays. Greg is a computer geek; there is not a computer or electronic system in the world he cannot access. He was originally a Navy pilot who did aircraft duty. He has nerves of steel. He also worked a few years in the Secret Service. You know, the guys who will take a bullet for the POTUS or whomever they are assigned to protect. You will shortly meet Henry Swenson. He and I go back a long way. We were college roommates. I'm normally the quiet person. Henry can be the life of the party when he turns it on. His nickname in college was Prince Harry because he looks a lot like Prince Harry from the UK. Henry is also a helicopter pilot and does fixed wing planes as well. Sometimes I think he believes he can just fly on his own. Henry can be a chameleon. Even though he is 5'10", he can blend into the background. That was necessary in our work with the Omega Team," said Reece.

"What is the Omega Team?" asked Sarah.

"Well, it's really classified, but since we are doing what we are doing, you're an honorary member. It's a small group under the leadership of Bruce Hardy. We report directly to the president of the United States. We did a lot of different assignments for the past president, Ralph Winston. The new president, President Sessions, sees no need for our team or the need for us to do anything special. So at this time we are a group without a portfolio," answered Reece.

"How do you work, and who pays you?" asked Sarah.

"We were always funded under the clandestine budget of the CIA. At this time we take assignments from the CIA or FBI as so asked," clarified Reece.

"I work for the CIA and have never heard of your group," said Sarah.

"That's the way we like it. We are literally licensed to kill. We arrange for accidental deaths, missing people, missing funds, missing equipment. You name it; when it has to happen in the best interest of the US government, we'll do it," said Reece.

"That sounds dangerous," observed Sarah.

"It is; or in my case, was. I retired a couple years ago," answered Reece.

"Talk about nerves of steel. Tell me about Jeff," asked Sarah.

"Jeff is the ultimate nerve of steel. He is a retired Navy Seal. By definition, you know he can do almost anything physically. He thinks he can fly like Henry but he does it underwater. We think he actually has gills. I have seen him swim fully loaded without showing any effort that anyone could notice. He seems to come up after an hour dive with more air in the tank than he started with. He can handle almost anyone in a hand-to-hand combat situation," continued Reece.

"No wonder he was able to overcome the perpetrator at the Detroit airport in what appeared to be child's play," commented Sarah.

"The challenge he had that we'll have is to not let the mind reading device give us away," retorted Reece.

"How did he do that?" asked Sarah.

"We'll use some of the same techniques. He had to think in terms of images and not words. He also had a hat that cut down the signals from his mind. Using that his approach was so fluid that it was almost impossible to take a defensive position. Sounds simple, doesn't it?" answered Reece.

"Greg seems to find these perpetrators out of thin air. How does he do that?" asked Sarah.

Reece took a big gulp of air and told Sarah, "First, as I just said, there is not a computer or a system that Greg cannot get into. In the United States we have been so occupied with security that there are cameras everywhere. They are on street corners, on highways, in stores, just about anywhere you can think.

Greg was able to tap into the license reading systems that most highways have now. Once he had the license plates of the three perpetrator cars he just let the existing system give him updates as to their locations. We thought we were going to have to use DNA to identify the perpetrators. As it happens, they are Chinese. The Chinese government has a very robust and exhaustive facial recognition system. Greg tapped in and let the Chinese government do the work."

"Ok, enough about your friends. Who and where did Reece Stanton come from? I have heard of your reputation in the halls at Langley. I know we worked together on the Senator's daughter but had no idea who you were," commented Sarah.

"Not much there. Just a boy raised on a dairy farm, milking cows, baling hay, worked from dawn to dusk," answered Reece.

"Continue, after you left the farm," said Sarah, trying to pull Reece out of his mysterious shell.

"Ok, went to college, studied engineering, of which Professor Quinn was one of my favorites instructors. I went into the Navy, since they don't have cows onboard ships. The work had to be easier. After that I was recruited to work for the CIA. Shortly after getting there, Bruce Hardy approached me, and the rest is history," answered Reece.

"Yeah, the history part is the lore in the halls. The rumor is that they already had a star for you on the wall three times, and each time you showed up to prove them wrong," said Sarah.

The stars on the wall of the CIA are unnamed for those lost in action while serving the country as a CIA operative.

"Yes, that's true. The rumors of my death are fortunately only that . . . rumors," said Reece with a smile from ear to ear.

"Your nickname is Ghost. Did you know that?" quipped Sarah.

"No, I don't believe I have heard that one," answered Reece.

"Well, that answers why you can get President Winston on the phone so easily," commented Sarah.

"My relationship with President Winston is actually very personal. I like and admire the man as much as anyone can. He is as all-American as can be," elaborated Reece.

"Thanks for all of that. Didn't hurt much, did it? Are we almost there for refueling? Are you sure the refueling plane will be there?" Sarah whined.

"Actually we are in a descent and going slower to engage soon," answered Reece.

About 15 minutes later, they were at the refueling altitude and speed. The KC-135Q suddenly showed up as if by magic.

Sarah let out a sigh of relief, "Oh, I never thought I would say a refueling plane was beautiful, but it is!"

As had happened after their takeoff, the skilled team on this KC-135Q extended the boom, connected to the SR-71, and filled their tank. It was over fairly quickly, and everyone signed off.

Once again Sarah and Reece headed to a higher altitude and much faster speed to the other end of Alaska on a heading of 54.77°. They would meet the next KC-135Q at Atta Island for the refueling that would get them to Okinawa. Atta Island is the western-most island in the Aleutian Islands. The flight was 45 minutes.

"Sarah, get ready, our last refuel is going to happen in about 15 minutes. We are slowing down and going down to the appropriate altitude. The crew in the plane will be as eager as we are to meet. They will have just enough range to get back once they unload the fuel on us," said Reece.

"You mean they have an extra incentive to be here on time?" asked Sarah.

"You betcha. There they are. Here we go again," answered Reece.

The fuel boom came down to the location behind Sarah. By now she was becoming more accustomed to this necessary ordeal. In about 20 minutes they were done. As soon as the transfer and disengagement was completed, the KC-135Q turned sharply to head home. In the meantime, Reece took the SR-71 up to altitude and up to full speed, now on a heading of 38.99°. This last leg to Okinawa would last one hour and fifteen minutes. So far, the military support has been absolutely superb.

"Sarah, just a little over an hour more and the SR-71 portion will be done," said Reece.

"What type of plane will the military have for us from Okinawa to Taipei?" asked Sarah.

"I'm not sure. Probably it will be a C-37A," answered Reece.

"Talk English, Reece!" exclaimed Sarah.

"Ok, the C-37A is the military version of the Gulfstream V," answered Reece. "Not a lot of headroom, but much more comfortable than this rocket ship."

"You mean I can get a Coke and a snack?" replied Sarah, with the first sign of a sense of humor.

"Yes, it's used for high-ranking military officers, congressional junkets, and other mucky-mucks. There will more than the standard coach snack," replied Reece.

Satisfied that it was soon to be over, Sarah settled back down as much as she could in the SR-71's cramped seat.

About an hour and fifteen minutes later, Reece and Sarah were approaching the runway at Kadena Air Force Base. Reece explained that they were going to deploy a parachute to help stop them in their landing. He said, "When it fully deploys there will be a jolt, so prepare for it."

"Bloody hell!" was once again uttered from the backseat. Sarah was also very relieved.

The Blackbird taxied to the designated hangar to once again not really exist.

The ground crew opened canopies and unhooked space suits and disengaged them from their seats. They were now done.

Reece realized it took only four and a half hours and to get halfway around the world. Wow. Talk about jet lag. It was now 4:30 a.m. local time.

Once out of the plane, Sarah and Reece were escorted to a C-37A for the flight to Taipei. The military was arranging entry and would make the trip relaxing. It would take about 45 minutes to make the flight. The crew aboard the military version of the Gulfstream were used to taking care of their passengers' needs. It was just that Agent Sarah Castle needed to recover from the SR-71 flight.

Off they left for an uneventful trip to Taiwan.

Taipei, Taiwan

The flight from Okinawa was just what Sarah needed for a reset. The crew had a variety of snacks and shrimp, sashimi, sushi, and tempura to satisfy her palate. Japanese cuisine was Sarah's favorite. It was also Reece's. All of the above was especially appealing to him, too.

"The tuna sashimi is especially delicious," commented Reece.

"Yes, that's good, but the salmon sashimi is equally as good." Sarah responded, smiling back, now in full joy.

"Sarah, you earned it. I know it was hard, but it was necessary to get here before James Wang does. If he comes into the hotel and we are already there, he will let his guard down with regard to us. The British element will also put him more at ease. Henry will follow him from the airport to make sure he does come to The Riviera Hotel as we expect him to. It will be tricky to find an intercept point in such a public place. I'm not certain if there was a protocol for them to activate to assure that they were all on their way or that they had been captured. We have to assume he is on full alert. Don't eat too much. As part of our cover, we'll have to be at the lobby breakfast buffet when James Wang arrives. The buffet is to die for. It's the best of any hotel I have ever stayed in," explained Reece.

"Well, there's time to be at ease before we have to be equally alert," said Sarah with a great sigh.

As the plane was finishing the 42-minute flight into Taipei's Taoyuan International Airport, Sarah asked Reece the plan upon arrival.

"We should be met at the airport by Henry. We'll go directly to The Riviera Hotel in downtown Taipei. It's about a 40-minute ride. We'll then let Henry go back to the airport and watch for James to arrive. We'll check into the airport as the English couple, supported by our passports. By using the Blackbird, we had to travel light. Henry should have another bag for us to support the image of a traveling couple. After checking in, we'll go the room to drop off the bags and then head down to the morning breakfast buffet. I hope you did not fill yourself up with what was on this flight," explained Reece.

"No, I'm fine," replied Sarah.

"Good. We'll be on the lookout for James' arrival. We need him to notice that we are there prior to his arrival."

"How will you do that?" asked Sarah.

"Henry will call the front reception desk and ask them to find us in the dining area. It's right off the lobby. It takes a few minutes to check in. You have to present your passport, and in the case of new clients, present a credit card. During that time, I'll be interrupting

James' check-in. He will notice us," continued Reece.

"Will he not read your mind when you come to the desk?"

"No, my antidote model has a countermeasure for the model he has. He will only hear a slight hum from me. He will misinterpret it as a system failure," answered Reece.

"What about me?" asked Sarah.

"You should be out of his range. If he does come into the breakfast area, be sure to remember to repeat the poem we discussed mentally. That should confuse him. Then start thinking in terms of pictures. Your floppy hat is also lined with a fine mesh to act as a Faraday barrier to reduce the signal from you brain," answered Reece.

The plane landed, and due to their arrival on a US military plane, they went into a different part of the airport. It was limited to dignitaries and government officials. After the immigration and customs clearance, Sarah and Reece headed to the main terminal to find Henry.

He was outside with a black car. Of course there were dozens of black Mercedes Benz cars with willing drivers to take passengers to Taipei. Henry would not stand out from the crowd of other cars. Although there was a line of cars hoping to pick up passengers in chronological order, Reece knew Henry would be around the corner where other black cars were waiting for passengers that were directed by "bird dogs" in the airport. The "bird dogs" worked with these cars to offer a break in price to arriving passengers to go to their cars. It was not less, just a ploy to direct business to their cars. Nothing that's dishonest, it's just aggressive marketing. Welcome to the Chinese culture.

As Sarah and Reece rounded the corner, Reece saw Henry. Henry was wearing white gloves, and looked the part of a limousine driver. They quickly got in the car and they were soon heading down National Highway 1 past the lighted columns along the highway. They were like the ones at the LAX airport entrance in Los Angeles except they were not vertical but at an angle. They continued onto National Highway 2 heading north to Taipei. The city of Taipei was actually directly east of the airport, but one of the things to remember in Taiwan is there is never a straight-line path from one point to another. If you took a taxi from The Riviera Hotel to the airport, you would get lost when the driver takes so many turns on the city streets that it would be dizzying for a passenger. Somehow the taxi always got there; it was a miracle.

They pulled up to The Riviera Hotel and the doorman came over to unload the luggage.

It was a good thing Henry had added a bag with some weight to what Reece and Sarah brought on the SR-71. They paid Henry as if he was just a car driver and went inside. The luggage now was under the command of the bellhop. They walked to the desk that was located directly near the door on the right side. Past the reception desk was the piano, some plantings, and the dining area. It was now 6:00 a.m., and breakfast was being served.

Reece and Sarah presented their passports and a credit card. The lady spoke perfect American English. Reece and Sarah greeted her with their British accents. They inquired about the breakfast. They were informed that it was now being served.

The bellhop took their bags up to their room. They followed and went in to "freshen up."

Reece figured that Henry had plenty of time to get to the airport to "greet" James. He would be arriving in the private aircraft section of the airport. A lot of the arrivals there had their own local transportation, but there would be a few black limousines like what Henry was driving. He should blend in with the rest of them.

"We'll hear from Henry when James arrives. James' ETA at the airport is about 8:25 a.m. He will probably arrive at the hotel an hour later. We should head down for breakfast at 9:20 to be in place when James comes into the hotel," Reece said to Sarah.

Taoyuan International Airport

As the Gulfstream G650ER was in its final approach, Lisa came to James and asked about Mr. Ellis. She had not seen him once on the slightly over 10-hour flight. That was a little unusual; but James kept telling her that he was either sleeping or preparing for the meeting. Lisa could be a problem if James did not come up with a reason that she would not see Mr. Ellis on the flight and then the arrival. James had some flunitrazepam in a vial. *"How can I convince Lisa to have a drink with me?"* thought James. *"I have to subdue her upon arrival so she will not alert the cockpit crew."*

"Lisa, can I have a Bloody Mary. Do we have time?"

"Sure, I can get one in time."

"I wish he had thought about that drink 15 minutes ago and not when we are so close to landing," thought Lisa.

"Get one for yourself too, Lisa. It was a long flight and you need to relax too. Besides, I don't feel like drinking alone," exclaimed James.

"I'm not sure I want one, sir," replied Lisa.

"OK. Can I have a couple of the chocolate croissants too?" answered James, now having to come up with another plan.

"Yes, I'll warm a couple for you," answered Lisa, now slightly annoyed with the flight approach activity.

After Lisa gave the two croissants to James, she then returned to the galley to continue the lock-down for landing. James then used the dropper to put two drops of flunitrazepam on one of the croissants.

After eating the croissant that was not doped, he said to Lisa, "Lisa, I can't eat the second one. It's all yours." James knew she was a chocoholic. This was one thing she could not pass up. Sure enough, she said she would only do it so it was not wasted.

"Oh, James, you know I can't say no to chocolate," said Lisa. She quickly consumed the croissant and returned to the galley.

It was obvious that they were on the path to landing, so she got into her seat quickly and buckled up.

"Great, just in time," thought James.

As the wheels touched down, James saw Lisa slump in her seat. She was now out.

As they approached the hangar for the plane, James got up and put a pillow under Lisa's head. Now it looked like she was just tired from the flight and drifted off to sleep.

After the landing check-off routine was done, the cockpit crew came out and saw Lisa asleep.

James explained that she was really tired and asked if she could sleep the last 30 minutes of flight.

"I told her to get some rest. I'll wake her in a few minutes after I check in on Mr. Ellis," explained James.

"OK, see you later," said Matthew Webb, the pilot.

"Sure, Matt. See you later, Chris," James said to the pilot and the copilot.

James figured they would not come and check on Lisa and would just get their own transportation to the hotel. They normally stayed at the City Suites Hotel that was five minutes away from the airport.

James then checked on his booty of diamonds. He'd hidden them in the safe cabinet Mr. Ellis had in his quarters. He then got off the airplane. He just had to meet with Fred and Peter at The Riviera Hotel and then head to Hong Kong with them to do the delivery to his boss, Harry Yeh. Then, after that, he would find someplace in the world he could enjoy the rest of his life as a very rich man. *"Thanks, Mr. Ellis! It was worth my few years of investment with you,"* thought James Wang.

James waited a few minutes before getting off the plane. He wanted to make sure both Matt and Chris had cleared immigration and customs before he showed up to go through.

As James came to the desk for entry, he felt a small twinge of anxiety because of the last few days. He had done this many times before and told himself, "*Relax, James. You have been here many times with Mr. Ellis. It's just a formality. They never question who he is or if he had anything to declare.*"

"Hello, long flight," said James with a slight smile. Smiling is not a normal activity in the Asian culture. However, James was still feeling nervous, and was acting as if he was an American.

"Yes, sir. It is. But your flight is not crowded or like the commercial accommodations," replied the agent.

"You're right. I should be grateful."

"Welcome to Taiwan," said the agent, stamping James' passport.

James headed out the building toward the line of limousines that would take him into Taipei.

"Riviera Hotel," James said curtly to the driver. He was not feeling friendly, but was now on full alert. He had not received a message from either Fred or Peter. They should have arrived ahead of him. He would have to check this out when he got to the hotel. James was so distracted he did not notice an American observing him leaving the building and getting into another limousine.

Henry was close enough to hear James tell the driver, "Riviera Hotel." Henry called Reece. "Reece, James is now on his way to the hotel. You were right, he is going to The Riviera Hotel. Be careful; he does not look like a particularly nice guy."

"He is not. He was directly responsible for the assassination of the vice president. I'm in Room 612. Come to the room when you get into the hotel. I'll be down in the lobby so James hears and sees me but I'll come up shortly after his arrival," replied Reece.

Taipei, Taiwan

While in the car on the way from the airport to the hotel, James tried to connect with both Fred and Peter. Neither of their phones was active. This was not like them. They are the best, and James was confident they could handle almost any situation. Because of this dilemma, James went into his obsessive-compulsive persona. He started looking at the driver and wondered, did James pick him, or did the driver seek James out. "*Hmmm. He did seek me out. I was out near the cars and he directed me to his car. I wish I had a gun now. There should be one at the hotel for me when I get there,*" thought James. Then he realized the directing to the car was normal for all the limousine drivers and their guides. It was a very competitive situation. They were all trying to land the next passenger. "*Still, I cannot relax until I know about Fred and Peter. If they failed, I have the only model for delivery. The boss will not be happy if that's the case,"* continued the thoughts James was fretting about.

As the car pulled up to The Riviera Hotel, the doorman opened the limousine door and welcomed James. Huānyíng," said the doorman to James.

James replied in English, "Thank you."

James went into the lobby. The check-in area was a small desk with a young lady sitting behind it. She requested James' passport, and courteously welcomed him to the hotel as an old friend, referring to him by name even before he presented the passport. James had been here many times before with Oliver Ellis. He could not help but smell the breakfast buffet as he sat down in the chair opposite the young lady. The small arrangement of floor plantings was the only barrier to aromas drifting from the dining area.

The clerk noticed James' head turn slightly toward the dining area of the first floor. She smiled and said, "Mr. Wang, as you know, we serve one of the best breakfast buffets in Taipei. Please help yourself after we finish the check-in. The bellhop will take your luggage to your room."

"Thank you. I'm famished. That sounds like a good idea," responded James. "*Finding Fred and Peter can wait.*"

After receiving his key card, James stood up and proceeded to the dining area. As he entered, he heard a charming laugh from a pretty British lady. He could tell by her delicate accent and the way she held the teacup before her. She was inquiring of her companion about the differences between Taipei and Hong Kong.

"Well, the topography is one big noticeable difference. Hong Kong is a series of hills, whereas Taipei is fairly flat, except along the western edge of the island. Hong Kong is integral to the water. Everything is close enough to the water to never forget it's there. In Taipei we are several kilometers away from the ocean. Shopping is similar in that almost everything is available. You will soon see for yourself. We'll try it in both cities." Reece carried on, making sure his voice was to Sarah but could be overheard. Reece was taking a gamble that ultimately James Wang would be going to Hong Kong after Taipei. If Reece was unsuccessful in Taipei, he had to indicate that he was going to also be in Hong Kong, as planning would have it. This conversation was plan B, since Henry did not call Reece to the desk while James checked in. Timing must have been the issue.

"Let us go up to our room and have a morning rest," quipped Sarah.

Off they went. They were certain that James made note of them and eliminated them as a threat. After all, they were from the UK and were here before he arrived.

Sarah and Reece got off the elevator on the fifth floor. There in the foyer off the elevator, sitting patiently, was Henry. All of them headed to Room 612 without saying a word. Now with the door closed behind them, "What did they do to the fourth floor?" asked Henry. Reece explained that four was an unlucky number in China, as 13 is in most of the United States.

"A lot of hotels skip designating a fourth floor. It's labeled five. This room is on the top floor and the fifth floor but labeled six," explained Reece.

"What's the plan?" asked Henry.

"You're the point guy. James is down having a breakfast. I heard the receptionist tell the bellhop to take James' luggage to Room 309. Thankfully, he is not on the same floor with us. We have to find out if he is alone. I suspect he was to meet both Fred and Peter here. Since they are not meeting him, he is going to be very wary. It's normal for people to sit in the lobby sitting area to read and relax. Go to the third floor and wait to see if James goes to his room alone. There is a sitting area, which many visitors use to read, talk, or relax. Wait to see if anyone joins him. Take a good, thick book. You have one, right?" replied Reece.

"*War and Peace* good enough?" asked Henry with a smile.

"Funny, but appropriate. Seriously?" answered Reece.

"No. It's actually *The Gulag Archipelago* by Aleksandr Solzhenitsyn," answered Henry.

"Oh, a very good second choice," laughed Reece.

"Do you really read that for enjoyment?" piped up Sarah with a giggle.

"Yes, as a matter of fact. It's a classic, and quite the read," answered Henry.

"Wow, what a teammate! I heard she was smart and good-looking. But this is exceptional. I sure would like to work with her more," thought Henry.

"I'm about one-third the way through so it does look like I'm reading it. See you later to report on the status," continued Henry.

"We got some goodies from Greg. Here is a bird I want you to launch from the exercise area on the roof. Here is the power switch," explained Reece.

"Wow, what's it for?" asked Henry.

"The guys who do *Spy in the Wild* for PBS make all kinds of these to observe animals with a robotic one that has a camera eye," explained Reece. "Greg got the pigeon so we can follow James if he leaves the hotel."

"Who's going to operate it?" asked Henry.

"When you have it ready for flight you have to call Greg. He'll operate it like a drone and let us know what's happening. It does have a limited battery life so when it's down on energy, Greg will return it to the roof. You'll have to go back up and change out the battery," Reece explained.

"I was wondering how we were going to monitor James without all the cameras that we have in the States," said Henry.

"Off you go," said Reece. "Oh, and Henry?"

"Yes?"

"Remember, I have one of the hearing devices in my ear. Understand? We are on a mission," said Reece.

"Yes, sir," said Henry with a slight blush, knowing that Reece had just read his mind about his attraction to Sarah.

"Have fun," Sarah said cheerfully as Henry went through the door with his book and small bag with the bird inside.

Henry took up residence in the third-floor sitting area. He was also in a room on the third floor so it was normal for someone to read in their floor's sitting area. The rooms are very nice but small for extended periods of time. The sitting area is open to a center atrium that goes from the lobby to a skylight in the roof. Henry had to wear his baseball cap with the integrated Faraday mesh to limit his thoughts getting to James Wang if he got close.

About 30 minutes later, James arrived on the floor and exited the elevator. It appeared that he did not pay attention to Henry. Henry was engrossed in his book to the casual eye. James went down the hall and to his room. James was trying to perceive any thoughts from this man. No thoughts came that were understandable.

"I guess he does not say the words as he reads," thought James.

***

James Wang went into his room. He thought, *"The man in the sitting area looks familiar to me. Did I see him at the airport?"* James was on high alert; he was trained to notice stature, as well as facial characteristics, and movement as well as biometric subtleties. People hold their heads or move their hands in a noticeable manner to the trained eye. It was this that made James think he saw this man near the limousine queuing station.

James then called his Taipei contact and asked for two helpers to meet him.

The man at the other end of the phone said to meet the men at the Taipei Datong District - Linsen Temple. The instructions were clear. Go out the front door of the hotel. Turn right and walk three blocks. Go to the third floor. Go to the bench as if to pray to the god of that floor. The men will recognize you. They are big. You will know them by that.

He was to leave in 20 minutes. James asked the contact on the phone if he had heard from either Fred or Peter. He had not. James was now alarmed. He thought, *"There was nothing on the news that any of the people behind the explosion or the assassination had been arrested. The international flight ban is still in effect."*

James came out of his room. The man reading the book was there. James pressed the elevator button and went to the lobby once it came.

As James got on the elevator, Henry called Reece. "James just got on the elevator."

"Good. Take the bird to the exercise area and release it," instructed Reece.

Henry took the elevator to the top floor and found the signs directing clients to the exercise area on the roof. Sure enough, after climbing a flight of stairs, Henry was now outside. There was a running track around the roof. A small, glass-enclosed room held stationary bikes and an assortment of other exercise equipment. Henry went to the far side of the track, took out the bird, and then called Greg.

"Greg, Henry here. Are you ready to take flight?"

"Sure am, buddy. Press the power button and I'll take it from there."

"OK, James is headed downstairs. I'm sure he's going to leave the building," said Henry.

Greg was actually excited to use the bird. He did get a chance to practice before it was put on the SR-71 with Reece and Sarah. However, this time it was showtime.

With Greg's instructions, the bird started to fly. It was miraculous. It flew as if it were a real bird. Over the side of the building it flew.

Greg spotted James coming out of the hotel door. James turned right and looked around as if to see if anyone was following him. Of course they were; but doing it with a robotic bird controlled from the other side of the world. *"Isn't technology wonderful?"* thought Greg as he maneuvered the bird to stay above James but not ahead of him.

After about a 10-minute walk, James was at the temple. It was an open structure. No windows, no doors. It was just a structure with lots of religious statues and symbols. It was actually very pretty.

James went up to the third floor. There were only stairs. He got to the open space with the idol for the floor. As he approached the idol as if to pray, two very large men came out of the shadows and put their hands on him. James was very skilled in Jūnshì Sǎndǎ. However, it would be a challenge to take them both on. Thank God he did not have to. James explained that he was waiting for Fred and Peter. If they didn't arrive by tomorrow morning he was to continue on to Hong Kong without them. He told them about the man who was reading a book on his floor. He now was certain that it was the same man who was at the airport. They needed to take care of him. They understood what James meant by take care of him.

Greg and the bird were watching and listening while the bird perched on one of the open spaces on the outside wall. It was a perfect ledge for a bird to sit unnoticed. Other birds came and sat next to it. What perfect camouflage! Greg had the conversation on an open communication link to both Henry and Reece. Henry was now a known target. When James came back to the hotel, he was going to start pursuing Henry.

The bird watched as the three men went down the stairs and proceeded back to the hotel. The bird followed. Greg watched as the three men entered the hotel. H flew the bird to the exercise area that was the launch site.

It was now close to noon. Reece and Sarah went down the stairs to have lunch in the hotel. As they came down on the elevator, James and his two new friends greeted them. They exchanged nods and traded places. James and his two associates took the elevator to the third floor, while Reece and Sarah went into the dining area and sat at a table next to the window that looked out onto the street.

Henry was to go to his room to retrieve a new battery for the bird and change it out. As he came out of his room, James and his two new friends were getting off the elevator. Henry pressed the button for an elevator to take him up to the top floor. Though he knew he was a target, he had to assume that his status as a target was not totally confirmed.

He got on the elevator and went up to the top floor. James and his two friends watched the elevator reach the top floor. The two men had also pressed for an elevator to take them up. It arrived, and they then proceeded to go to the top floor too. When they got out, they looked around for where the target went to. As they searched, the only option was one of the rooms or . . . they walked around a set of stairs indicating exercise area. The other elevator was still on the floor.

Henry was a little concerned now. He went up the stairs to the exercise area. There, sitting on the ledge was the bird, waiting for him. He approached the bird, picked it up and removed the battery pack. From his bag he retrieved a new battery and inserted it. He then called Greg and told him that the bird was now online for its next mission.

"Greg, you know me, but I'm a little spooked. I just saw the guys who are going to take care of me on the way up here," said Henry.

"Relax, Henry. I have your back," said Greg.

"Yeah? Does the bird have a hidden gun under its wing?" asked Henry.

"Sorry, buddy. All I can give you is a little moral support. Now get back to your room and figure out a way out of the country, since you have been made."

Just as they both said goodbye, out of the stairwell arrived James' two new best friends. Henry realized he was close to the ledge and knew he had to get by them to the stairwell. One guy stood his ground and the other came like a jaguar onto that evening's meal. Henry was very much in shape, and at 5'10" no wilting flower. Henry realized he was no match for this guy though. When his buddy came over, Henry realized he was now going to be taken care of. As they easily lifted him, they were going to see how well he could fly. In a matter of seconds, Henry was over the ledge and on his way to the pavement below.

There was a loud thump just above the sidewalk next to where Reece and Sarah were having lunch. Two tables over was James, by himself. The loud thump turned into a tearing of cloth. Something had hit the fabric awning on the hotel's window. Then, coming through the newly ripped blue-and-white-striped awning, was the body of Henry Swenson. Everyone in the dining area watched as the man fell to the concrete sidewalk. Blood was now spreading over the sidewalk. The man was still alive, but was moaning from the pain and injury due to the fall. A hush went through the room. All eyes were fixated upon the plight of this man. James was watching all the people in the dining area to determine if there was a connection between anyone around him and the man on the sidewalk. No one moved as if he was a friend. Reece looked at Sarah and she looked at him. Both knew instantly this was a test to smoke out any other collaborators. Both Reece and Sarah had to stay in character. This was the big league. A mission has to take priority over everything.

They covered their mouths in shock like everyone else and looked at the waiter and staff. Soon many people were on the sidewalk trying to assist Henry. He was moving limbs and moaning. He'd survived the flight from the roof. It was obvious that was how James wanted Henry to be taken care of. Reece was now mad at himself for not having Henry immediately leave the hotel before James returned once they knew he had been made.

It was taking all her training for Sarah to control her thoughts. She realized that James may be able read her mind despite the floppy hat she was wearing with an imbedded wire mesh. Reece had his countermeasures model that scrambled his thoughts, so James was unable to understand what Reece was thinking.

Reece could hear the mind of James. He was thinking, *"Stupid. The guys were to throw him off the roof directly onto the concrete sidewalk. They should have examined for any fall-breaking elements like the obvious blue-and-white-striped awning. Now the person will live. However, he is not going to be on my tail. I don't see anyone around here reacting as if they know him. I just can't believe he was alone. But then again, how did he get here before me? Before they get anyone else here I'll be in Hong Kong. I'll leave for Hong Kong tomorrow morning."*

Reece thought, *"After we get done here, I have to share this with Sarah. So far the floppy hat she is wearing is masking any thoughts she may have. We probably should leave for Hong Kong this afternoon so as to be there once again before James. I suspect his guard is going to be really intense while in Taipei. Hong Kong should be a more relaxed environment for him."*

About five minutes later, an ambulance was on the scene with police and first responders. They carefully lifted Henry, put him on a gurney, and whisked him away. Greg had watched the events of the men on the roof grabbing Henry like he was a play toy and tossing him over the ledge. The bird had followed him down and observed from a tree nearby as the events unfolded. Greg made the executive decision to contact Jacob Smith at the FBI so he could alert the Taiwanese people that a person of very high importance to the US government was now injured and on his way to a hospital.

"Smitty, this is Greg Mays. We have a situation in Taipei you need to help us on. One of our guys, Henry Swenson, was just tossed off the roof of a building. He appears to be alive but is injured. Without my explaining how I followed the ambulance to the hospital, it's a short distance from The Riviera Hotel. It's the MacKay Memorial Hospital at No.92, Sec. 2, Zhongshan N. Rd., Zhongshan District, Taipei City 104. The telephone number there is 2543-3535. Please arrange for someone from the embassy to be there and run interference. Also, we need to make sure he is safe from another attack on his life," blurted Greg.

"Wow, no hi, Smitty, how are you? You guys are really wired. I got it. We'll take care of Henry for you. How is Reece? Has his cover been blown?" asked Jacob Smith, the FBI director.

"No, I think both Reece and Sarah having set up a ruse of being there ahead of him was a good idea. I don't know how they could watch Henry fall and get injured without reacting. They truly are professionals, and realized the mission was over if James saw them react," answered Greg. They both hung up knowing there was a lot of pressure on Reece and Sarah.

Both Sarah and Reece finished their lunch and stopped at the front desk as any concerned person would do and inquired as to the status of the person who fell to the sidewalk. The clerk did not have any news.

They then went to their room. Inside, they opened up.

"I heard James thinking while he watched Henry come off the roof. He was ticked off at his guys for not considering the awning. He wanted Henry dead. These guys play for keeps. He also does not suspect us. He was observing the dining area to see if there was a reaction by anyone indicating they knew the man on the sidewalk. You did an excellent job. He is leaving for Hong Kong tomorrow morning. He is on high alert now. To make another move on him in Taipei is not a good idea. We need to get there before he does. We'll leave this afternoon. Somehow, we have to let James know that we are headed to Hong Kong before him," said Reece.

"Let me go downstairs and let the desk clerk know we are checking out this afternoon, while indicating we're continuing on to Hong Kong. James Wang is still probably downstairs watching for anyone who may be linked with Henry," said Sarah.

"Sounds good. Let me check in with Greg," said Reece as Sarah walked out the door. "Hi, Greg. Our man here is spooked. He's going to be in Hong Kong tomorrow."

"Let me check to see if he has a reservation at a hotel in Hong Kong . . . Got it! James is going to stay at the Harbour Grand, which is at No. 23 Oil Street. Now let me get you a reservation there too, as well as flights to

Hong Kong this afternoon," replied Greg. After a few brief moments he returned. "Done and done. You have flights, texting it to you. Also hotel reservations, I'll text that to you as well."

"We need to retrieve the bird robot," commented Reece.

"There's a car repair shop across the street on the corner from your hotel. It's an open shop. Walk in with the duffle bag; the bird will fly in the shop and hop into the bag. Just open it wide," answered Greg.

"You want me to do it now?" asked Reece.

"Yes, do it now."

When Reece got downstairs, he noticed James Wang watching the people entering and leaving the hotel. He was looking for someone to consider as another threat. He was using the mind reader to observe the thoughts of the people as they came and went. It was obvious that Sarah had been successful in feeding

James's mind that Sarah and Reece were now on their way to Hong Kong.

"Sarah, just going out to pick up something. I'll be back soon," Reece said to Sarah and went out the front door.

"OK," replied Sarah.

Reece walked across the street and entered the car repair shop. The mechanic did not look up, since the potential customer did not come into the shop with a car. As Reece entered, he left his duffle bag near the door with the mouth open. He went into the shop. As he entered he heard the man talking on the phone in English to a customer about the job being finished the next day. Reece knew he could engaged the mechanic in a conversation of his experience with working on BMW cars. The German car company had deeply penetrated the Taipei and Hong Kong markets. He knew that service was important. The mechanic professed to be able to service this potential customer's BMW.

"What model do you have?" asked the mechanic.

"I have an X-5," answered Reece. Not lying. He had one at home. It just happened to be on the other side of the world.

"Are you having problems?" asked the mechanic.

"No, just finding out if you could be an option for general maintenance," answered Reece.

Out of the corner of his eye, Reece watched the bird fly in the shop and hop into the bag. Reece had positioned himself so the mechanic could not see the duffle bag and the bird getting into it.

"Thank you for your time," said Reece. He then turned and left with his duffle bag. He crossed the street and went up to his room. With James Wang in the observing position in the lobby, Reece had no option except to nod his head and say a greeting of hello in Chinese, "Nǐ hǎo." Reece realized that James Wang was unable to hear his thoughts. This might be a problem because James was on alert. However, some people don't think as they walk from one location to another. Reece got into the elevator quickly.

When Reece entered their room he saw Sarah sitting, waiting with the suitcases packed. Not that there was much to pack.

They then went down the elevator and went to the payment window to pay for their stay.

Reece and Sarah had to let James Wang hear that he would see them again.

"Where are we staying in Hong Kong?" asked Sarah, noting that she was within earshot of James.

"One of my favorites, the Harbour Grand. It has one of the most elegant lobbies in all of Hong Kong. You'll love it. We have a room overlooking the harbor," answered Reece, again making sure James could hear.

They had a taxi come up to the entrance, wherein the bags were put into the trunk and they got into the car.

The trip to the Taipei airport was a short one.

The flight was only an hour and 45 minutes to Hong Kong. It's a beautiful city from the air. The city is a number of islands with the typical topography; hills and steep inclines. From the air it looked like there was not a square inch of undeveloped land. It was filled with extremely tall buildings and a variety of other structures.

The Harbour Grand was everything Reece had told her it was. The lobby was cavernous. The height went for two, maybe three stories. At one end of the lobby was a magnificent staircase, with a harp on a landing near the top of the stairs. It made her think of the stairs of the temple at Chichen Itza near Cancun, Mexico. Stairs that seemed to go up to the heavens.

When Sarah and Reece had finished checking into the hotel and got to their room, Reece took a new device out of his "magic bag." That's what Sarah was calling the bag Greg had put into their luggage that was filled with surprises. It was the bag from which Reece had retrieved the robot bird. This time Reece took out a small, VERY small, device. It was a bee!

"Does that do what I think it does?" asked Sarah.

"You betcha. A special present from Greg," answered Reece.

"How does it work?"

"Same as the bird. Greg will control it and keep us informed. Greg has also enabled the ability for us to view the action the bee sees on our iPhones," answered Reece.

"Why the bee and not the bird?" asked Sarah.

"Because there are fewer birds around here, and certainly not within the buildings. Our task is to retrieve the mind reader device, stop the perpetrator, and also find out the identity of the client. The bee will have to assist us in the retrieval of the mind reader device," Reece explained. "Now off to a fine Hong Kong restaurant for us. Tomorrow, it will all happen."

***

Meanwhile, James Wang was slightly off his game. He was disappointed that the person the men threw off the roof survived. A loose end; but at least he was now out of action. The British couple was tickling his self-preservation instincts. Taken at face value, it would not make sense that they were always one step ahead of him and at the same locations. He was considering changing hotels in Hong Kong except his boss had already made reservations, and he particularly liked the Harbour Grand. *"I guess this is just one of those times that coincidences are just that. I have to be wary of real threats, not imagined ones. Besides, if someone is after me, they would not be so obvious in their presence. I'm now really concerned about Fred and Peter,"* thought James.

James confirmed with his boss, Henry Yeh, that he had the mind reading unit. He confirmed to Henry that the unit functioned as they had been led to believe. You could just stand there and listen to people think as if they were talking. "It's just amazing how easy it works," James told his boss. "The client will be very happy with the delivery."

"What is not going to make the client happy is that the other two are still in the missing category. I have not heard from either Fred or Peter. There is nothing in the

American news about them being captured. The entire country is still in a lockdown, so they don't know about you," said Henry Yeh.

"I'm not sure about that. I had a person who was trailing me. I saw him at the airport and then at my hotel," responded James.

"What did you do about him?"

"I had a couple guys throw him off the top of a building."

"Did you do that on a hunch?"

"Yes. That's how I have made it this far in life. I have a good intuition about protecting myself," explained James.

"Too bad for him being in the wrong place at the wrong time," replied Henry.

"Better him than me."

"Right. See you tomorrow."

"I'll fly Oliver Ellis' plane to Hong Kong. Will you meet me at the airport?" asked James.

"Yes, text me when you depart."

***

The MacKay hospital a few blocks from The Riviera Hotel was abuzz with the normal duties. The man who fell at the hotel was now in the surgery center after getting x-rays and CAT scans to determine what was broken and what was damaged.

Several members of the American embassy were waiting for an update from the attending physician. The lead person from the embassy, Michelle Dent, had informed the hospital that the man brought in from the fall at The Riviera Hotel was an important person to the government of the United States of America. The receptionist informed Ms. Dent that Dr. Zhào would be out soon to brief them on his condition.

After five minutes, Dr. Zhào appeared. He had just examined the results of the x-rays and CAT scans.

Dr. Zhào stated to the small group, "If this man was not in perfect physical condition, we would have a lot more to fix here."

"What is his status?" asked Michelle. She was a rather short woman with light-brown hair and brown eyes. Despite her small stature, it was obvious she was always in charge of what was around her.

Dr. Zhào said, "He broke his left arm. It appears to have broken his fall to the awning and then was the first to hit the sidewalk. There are no internal injuries. I would have thought he would have broken a leg. However, his muscular legs saved him. He is bruised on his left side from the fall. He somehow kept his head up, which did not hit the cement sidewalk. He must have had training on how to take a fall and minimize the injuries."

"Thank you, Doctor," said Michelle.

"Well, if you will excuse me, I have to go into the surgery center and set that arm," said Dr. Zhào.

"One last thing, Doctor. When can we expect for him to be able to travel?" asked Michelle.

"I would like a couple days to make sure there are no other complications and see if he can handle the pain of the broken arm," answered Dr. Zhào.

Dr. Zhào said goodbye and went into the surgery center.

Talking to his colleagues in the room, Dr. Zhào noted, "Wow, anyone else would have several broken limbs and head trauma. I suspect he was trained for this. Let's set the arm and make sure there are no other injuries the man has suffered."

As Henry was being given anesthesia to put him out, he asked the attending doctor where he went to medical school. His reply of internal medicine residency at Stanford Medical School was the last thing he heard.

After about 60 minutes, Henry Swenson was on his way to a private room with a couple of windows and sunshine. He ached all over, but was happy for his training. Even with that, he probably would not have survived if it had not been for the awning. The impact on the awning told him that he had a chance. He hit with one side of the body to absorb the impact. He arched his head up to make sure it did not take the initial impact. It was reflex and training that made him do that. His pain drug of choice, morphine, was liberally being administered. He knew he would not get hooked on it but enjoyed what it was doing to reduce the pain from all his injuries. The doctor had told him the only significant injury, aside from the bruises, was a broken arm.

Henry was asleep in a few minutes. When he awoke some two hours later, there stood three people. The short woman got up from the chair she was sitting in when she saw Henry's eyes open.

"Hi, my name is Michelle Dent. I'm from the US embassy. The director of the FBI called me personally to make sure you were being fully take care of. Either I or someone from the embassy will be here until you can go home," said Michelle.

Weakly Henry replied, "Thank you."

"It's our pleasure. It takes real horsepower to get a direct call from the head of the FBI. I'm impressed. The president next time?" said Michelle with a smile.

"That can be arranged if you want. But, thank you for being here. Is that a jarhead over there in the corner?" Henry smiled, knowing that a call from the president actually could be arranged.

"Yes, he is. Please, not two calls like that in one week," pleaded Michelle. She was not sure if that was the level of this man's reason for being in Taiwan.

After having a couple sips of water, Henry went back to sleep. He was now safe.

Washington, DC

The White House was still in turmoil because the status from Greg was filtered through the FBI. The decision was made that the US could lift the air traffic ban. The traveling public, the airlines, and the corporate world were all relieved. The airlines had a full system functioning very quickly. The international flights were the only ones that had been restricted. Those were the moneymakers for the airlines, and they wanted to be back in business as soon as possible.

The press secretary came out to the podium. "Welcome. We have intercepted the perpetrators of the assassination of the vice president. There will more information on that later. However, I'm here to announce that we have lifted the international flight ban. Flights will be operating as soon as the airlines can accommodate this change. Check with your airline regarding their flight availability."

The press secretary turned and quickly left the room as many of the White House Press Corps shouted their questions to a vanishing press secretary.

CHAPTER NINE

Saturday

It was now Saturday morning in Taiwan. The sun was shining. The weather in the fall can be unpredictable, but this day was to be a nice fall day for the people of the island of Formosa. That was the name of the island, which was Portuguese for Beautiful Island. It is a beautiful island, with mountains along the length of the western side down to the slopes of the Taiwan Strait on the east shore. It was 81 to 140 miles from mainland China, depending where you measured.

James had now decided that he was not under pursuit. He had heard that the US had lifted the international ban on flight. They must think they have the people they want. Once again, he had accomplished the task he was assigned. He was still worried about Fred and Peter, but he knew he was the hero for Henry Yeh. They were to meet with the client later this afternoon.

James called the crew to have them take him to Hong Kong. He had to explain that Mr. Ellis was going to stay in Taiwan while James was doing other business for the boss in Hong Kong. James had decided that when he got to Taiwan, he was going to leave the diamonds onboard while in Taiwan. He did not want to bring them into the country and then out again. He had texted his boss, Henry Yeh, as he was leaving Taiwan.

***

"James, I apologize about falling asleep when we landed in Taipei," said Lisa Carter.

"That's OK. Mr. Ellis said that his running around the world was not fair to you. He said when he got off the plane to let you sleep. Did you see the note he had me leave?" said James.

"That was a smart move to prolong the concept that Mr. Ellis had made the trip," thought James.

"Yes, that was kind of him. He really is a good man to all of us," commented Lisa.

"Yes, he is," replied James, now relieved that he did not kill Mr. Ellis. He had been good to all that he dealt with on a personal level.

In about two hours, James had cleared Hong Kong immigration and customs and was on the curb waiting for Henry Yeh.

"You made it in fast time," commented Henry when James got into the back of the black limousine.

"Sure is easy with Oliver Ellis' jet. I'll miss that," responded James.

"We can have lunch, and then we'll meet the client on his yacht in the harbor."

Henry Yeh could not control himself. He started thinking so James would tell him what he was thinking. *"James you did a good job. However, we just have to turn over the device to our client. Are you ready for that?"*

"Yes, I am," responded James.

"Wow, it does work!" exclaimed Henry.

"Yes, it does."

**

The early morning sun was brilliant. Sarah had never been to Hong Kong. She was mesmerized by the hustle and bustle of the city/state. Reece explained the strategy to get James to remove the hearing device and take it as an accident. The bee would watch James come into the hotel and follow him to his room. It would identify who he meets with and record the meetings he would have.

Reece explained the sequence, stressing that the timing was very important.

"It's going to be a combination of disorientation, lots of visual input, sound input, and an attack by a crazy bee that will be confronting James. The bee has an annoy mode that Greg will execute just as James passes you at the harp. The bee will buzz his face and avoid being swatted away. I saw it in action. It's a marvelous piece of software. The bee is having fun with you while you're trying to not get stung. Your harp playing will fill the lobby with pulsating music. The bee will attack James' face. Meanwhile, I'll put the hearing device into the high screeching mode. As he removes the hearing device to stop the painful noise, I'll trip him and grab the device from his hand as he starts to fall. My grabbing the device will feel and appear as an attempt to prevent him from the fall. I'll actually be pushing him down the steps. By the time he gets to the bottom step he will have forgotten that I was on the steps. It's then that he will realize he no longer has the hearing device in his ear," explained Reece.

"That's cool. Do you really think we can pull it off?" asked Sarah.

"Yes, however it will be equally important that we quickly disappear so we are not considered to be a part of his falling or the loss of the hearing device. As he is falling I'll get to you, and we'll quickly go up the stairs to the elevator."

"How did you know I played the harp?"

"Your file indicates that you play the harp and piano. That was great, since we were not sure which was going to be set up in the hotel."

"What else do you know about me from that file?" asked Sarah a little tentatively.

"Well, you're a big fan of Madeline Arney from Franklin, Kentucky. I agree, she is amazing, especially considering her age. How about playing Pachelbel's Canon? Everyone stops and listens to that. It captivates all when it's played," answered Reece.

"I can do that. It's one of my favor pieces of music, too," replied Sarah.

***

It was now just before noon when James and Henry Yeh got to the hotel. They checked in at the desk. Neither noticed the small flying insect. This bee was different. It could not only fly, but it had a camera for an eye, a communication link that relayed to a satellite, and a remote control system. The computer on board was based upon nanotechnology. It was a brilliant marvel. It also had some onboard subroutines to make it follow a target, buzz a target, and penetrate a small orifice.

After they checked in, they went to their separate rooms and agreed to come down in 30 minutes to meet and then have lunch with the client on his yacht outside the harbor. The bee followed James. When he went into his room, the bee followed.

Greg was watching as James washed his face and put on a fresh shirt. James was humming with delight. His prior demeanor of impending danger was now put at ease. He was done. He was to be a hero to his boss, Henry Yeh. He was also now a wealthy man. He was happy to be in Hong Kong. Along with Antwerp, London, Tel Aviv, and Dubai, Hong Kong was a hub for the diamond business. He would cash in enough to go to a place to hide from the rest of the world. If he cashed in $10 million of diamonds, no one would blink an eye. A $10 million transaction was just another day in the world of diamond trading in Hong Kong.

Henry Yeh called and told James he was downstairs waiting for him.

"I'll be right there," James said as he snapped out of his dream of being rich.

James decided to come down the high stairs as if to make a grand entrance. Again the bee was following. Meanwhile, with the heads-up notice from Greg, Sarah took her position at the harp on the landing. Reece was at the foot of the stairs on the lobby floor. As James started down the stairs, he was a little surprised to see Sarah playing the harp. She was playing Pachelbel's dramatic Canon in D flat. The music filled the cavernous lobby. Everyone was watching this pretty lady playing such a dramatic piece of music with such passion. James even felt the passion as she played. As he passed her he nodded in recognition that their paths had crossed before. Just as he passed Sarah, James saw the lady's husband coming up the stairs toward her.

As James started the first step below the harp landing, Reece activated the mind reader remote kill button. This created a screeching sound in James' ear.

As James got down three steps, his left ear was no longer filled with music but with an extremely loud screeching sound that was both distracting and painful. It was the hearing device. It must be malfunctioning! All James could consider was getting it out of his ear to ease the pain. As he was pulling on the retrieving string to remove the device, he was getting attacked around his head by a bee. With his right hand he started to swat the bee for it to leave his face alone.

As Reece was on the step below James, he hesitated and put a foot in James' path. James was so distracted he did not even see Reece. Reece was on James' left side. With one swift move he grabbed the mind reading device from James' hand and helped James fall on the steep stairway. James continued to tumble all the way down to the lobby floor.

James was rolling down the remaining steps like a log. He tried to stop the continuing fall with his arms to no avail. He had enough momentum that he slid on the marble floor to a planter further in the lobby.

It was not the least bit elegant. As he stood up he saw his boss, Harry Yeh, approach him, first questioning how he was.

Immediately, James realized he was no longer able to read his boss' mind. Quickly James thought, "*Where is the device? Did it fall with me? Did it bounce along the polished, hard marble floor? Is it under one of the planters? Is it still on one of the steps?*"

"James, what is that look of surprise?" asked Harry Yeh.

"I lost it!" screamed James in horror.

"What did you lose?"

"The device!"

"How? It was in your ear!" asked Harry in disbelief.

"It started to malfunction and started to painfully screech in my ear," explained James. "I pulled it out just before I fell down the stairs."

In their excitement, neither James nor Harry noticed that the harp had stopped playing and the British couple had disappeared. They had quickly proceeded up the stairs to their room. Reece had the device in hand. Meanwhile Greg, with the help of the bee, was now observing the horror and panic taking place in the hotel lobby.

"We'll be picked up by the client in a few minutes!" said Harry in halting words, based upon his horror of what was going to happen next.

"We just have to postpone the meeting and find the device," said James, trying to compose himself.

"Let's look everywhere on the floor."

"Ok, we have the next few minutes. Maybe we'll find it. You say it was emitting a loud sound. Let's try to hear it," said Harry, trying to calm himself.

For the next ten minutes they searched everywhere on the floor of the lobby. They looked in the lobby planters in the event it went flying through the air as he fell. Neither James nor Harry made the connection of the absent British couple and the lack of music to the missing stolen device.

Meanwhile, Greg was observing the action, all within view and being heard by the robotic bee. Since Greg had enabled the system to relay the same visual and audio data to Reece and Sarah's iPhones, they watched and listened in the panicked search for the device that was now in Reece's hand. The plan was to destroy it immediately. He knew James and Harry Yeh would kill them to retrieve the recovered device. To keep it without destroying it would put their lives in danger.

Sarah observed Reece first put the hearing device into a vise-type box. As he closed the box, the hearing device was crushed. Then he opened a glass vial.

"What are you doing?" asked Sarah.

"Taking a precaution that we'll not be killed by either James or his boss," answered Reece as he dropped the crushed advanced technological device into the acid in the vial. The damage was done within a matter of seconds.

"If we still had that, and either James or his boss knew we had it, they would torture and/or kill us to get the operating system," continued Reece.

"What about the one in your ear?"

"They don't know about that one."

The action was now changing in the hotel lobby. The client's agent came into the lobby and asked Harry and James to follow him out to the limousine.

They followed as directed. The request was said as a command. Of course, the bee got into the car as they opened the doors. The bee settled in the foot well next to the driver in the front so as to not be visible.

It took ten minutes to ride from the hotel to the waiting water taxi that belonged to the yacht. It took another 25 minutes to get to the 350-foot yacht just outside Hong Kong Harbor. A Russian oligarch owned it. The bee was able to get out of the limousine onto the water taxi with the client's agent and the two Chinese perpetrators. During the ride from the hotel and then on the water taxi, neither James nor Harry said a word. The looks on their faces said it all. *"How do you tell a big-time client like this man that you were unsuccessful? What is he going to do to us? Maybe Fred or Peter made it here before us,"* thought James.

They could see the client on the boat as they approached the yacht. He was on an aft outdoor lounge that protruded over the water, throwing something overboard for entertainment. As they got closer, it became apparent that he was throwing fish overboard. In the water below were a large number of sharks, swimming around in circles. They were competing for the chum being thrown to them.

James and Harry carefully exited the water taxi onto the aft deck on the fantail of this enormous vessel. From there they were escorted to the deck on the side of the ship that projected over the water.

"Welcome to my home on the sea," said the client with a smile and a cheerful joy to his voice.

"Fred or Peter did make it here! He has two models. Ours was not necessary," thought James as he took the greeting at face value.

"Hello, Vladimir," said Harry, still not comfortable. He knew the client would not take failure lightly.

"Tell me what I'm thinking," asked Vladimir, in the belief that one of the two had the mind reading device in place.

"Vladimir, we are unable to do that right now," said Harry.

"Why not?" asked Vladimir.

"We had it in the hotel but it slipped out of James' ear in the hotel lobby when it started to malfunction," answered Harry.

"Did you look for it?" asked Vladimir in disbelief.

***

As this tense meeting was taking place, Sarah and Reece were leaving the hotel to make sure James never made the connection and found them. They were in the taxi on the way to the airport before James and Harry Yeh reached the water taxi. They were through the airport and were on the private jet sent by the military to pick them up and take them to Taipei by the time James and Harry were on the large yacht owned by Vladimir.

When they got on the military jet, both Sarah and Reece let out a sigh of relief. They were glued to their iPhones. What played before their eyes was what appeared to be an impossible meeting of James and his boss, Harry Yeh, with their client, Vladimir. They both knew that if they had the tables turned, both James and Harry would have killed them without remorse.

***

"You have been unsuccessful in the project. I don't put up with failure. You both have to pay the price," said Vladimir while nodding to the four large men standing near James and Harry. Both James and Harry were now being held in place by their arms by the men. There was not a thing either well-trained in Jūnshì Sǎndǎ man could do. Each Russian on each arm weighed twice the weight of James and

Harry. Their eyes widened with fright. This fear increased when they watched Vladimir take a Glock from his waistband.

"This is what happens when you fail me," Vladimir said as he shot James in one leg. He then shot Harry in both arms. The blood was pouring from both men. Vladimir must have hit an artery in each man. Blood was quickly covering the protruding deck. The deck was now slippery with blood.

As both James and Harry convulsed in pain and fear, the four large Russians picked up the two Chinese agents and easily threw them overboard. As they hit the water, both men flailed their arms, which only further attracted the circling sharks that were accustomed to finding food thrown from the boat. The screaming in Chinese was deafening. Vladimir said, "No one fails me." He turned to his people without a sign of remorse.

The blood covered the water in a hundred-foot-diameter circle in moments. The screams ended within one minute. Vladimir was still furious. Their deaths did not satisfy his disappointment. It was the Chinese who had approached him with the assignment. He thought to himself, *"There were devices that they had. Where are they? They said they had them when they assassinated the US vice president. James was their lead man in the US; he would not have come to Asia without the unit. I want to find it."*

Vladimir said to one of his helpers, "Take me ashore. I'll check the lobby myself."

Greg was listening. Greg was relieved; now the bee had a ride back to Hong Kong. He could retrieve it in a number of ways. Sarah and Reece had left. He had to contact the embassy and let someone with the sufficient classified clearance know that a bee would be entering their life.

***

Vladimir and his band of helpers descended upon the hotel. The staff at the hotel had already moved on from the incident earlier. Vladimir went to the front desk and related to the desk clerk about the guest falling down the stairs. The desk clerk responded in the affirmative, without many details. Vladimir indicated that the man was carrying something very small that seemed to have been lost in the fall.

"Could you show me were the guest was when he started his fall, and where he landed?" Vladimir said very curtly.

"Yes, sir. This way," answered the clerk.

They headed up the stairs to a couple steps below the harp landing.

"This is where I think he started to fall. Is your friend OK? Does he intend to sue the hotel?" asked the clerk. The clerk now realized his employer could be responsible for any injuries.

"He is not interested in such things. No, he will not take action against the hotel," answered Vladimir.

"Fine. Your friend tumbled down the stairs like a log down to the bottom. He tried to stop the rolling action with his arms, but he had too much momentum," explained the clerk. "He slid on the floor to that planter, which stopped his fall.

Vladimir's men then examined each step and the floor to the planter. They examined the planters in the area in the event the device went flying in the air.

After 15 minutes of effort, Vladimir told everyone they would leave and return to the yacht.

Vladimir was not done about losing such a device.

***

When the plane landed in Taipei, both Reece and Sarah let out another a big sigh of relief. They looked at one another and both laughed. It was just starting to dawn on them they were no longer at risk. With a smile Reece said to Sarah, "The military will return the SR-71 back to the US without our help."

Sarah hit him as she said, "That's good, because I would pay for my own ticket home if that was the case, and you would be flying it back alone."

Reece got serious and said, "Let's go to the hospital and see if Henry can be released."

"Good idea."

Sarah and Reece walked up to MacKay Hospital, not really knowing how bad Henry's condition was. Henry had been in the hospital only one day. Greg was to make commercial airline reservations for them the following day.

"You look better than you looked yesterday on the sidewalk. Next time, take the elevator," said Reece.

"Not my choice. I feel much better. A bit sore and aching over all over," responded Henry.

Dr. Zhào entered the room and said, "I have never seen such a fast recovery in my life. You certainly have good genes; and your being in great shape has paid big dividends for you. I would really like to have you stay another day for observation. Your friends could enjoy the shopping in Taipei. You must see Taipei 101 before you leave this fine city."

"And a good restaurant, too," piped up Sarah.

"Aw, I just get hospital food," said Henry with a smile.

As soon as the doctor left the room, Reece turned to Sarah and said, "OK, Taipei 101 it is. However, we'll find another hotel, in case

James' friends who helped Henry off the roof are out there looking for revenge. I'm sure they know by now that James and Harry Yeh are no longer part of the organization," said Reece.

After visiting with Henry for another hour, Sarah and Reece left the hospital. They took the short taxi ride to Taipei 101. Sarah was amazed that all the international big-name stores were there: Tiffany, Versace, De Beers, Gucci, and more than she could remember. Of course, first-class restaurants were also in the facility. This was her kind of one-stop shopping.

Reece took a chance while having a beer and thought he would call Greg. "Hi, Greg. Mission accomplished."

"Having a beer, Reece?" quipped Greg, knowing what his buddy did as a release after a mission.

"You betcha," laughed Reece.

"Did you get my bee back?" asked Greg, knowing full well that Sarah and Reece left Hong Kong before the bee made it off the yacht. "Remember, you signed it out."

"No, you did. I only brought it with me as a stowaway on the plane," replied Reece.

"Don't worry. I have a plan that involves it getting to the US embassy," said Greg.

Changing his tone, Greg asked, "How is Henry? Ready to travel?"

"We checked in with him on the way here. He'll be ready tomorrow. Get us all seats in something slower than an SR-71," answered Reece.

"Will do. Coach OK?" Greg smiled as he said it.

"Ha ha, spend the big bucks and get us back in style," retorted Reece. "Got to go. I have to call Tori and let her know I'm alive and coming home."

"Don't worry, buddy. I've been letting Tori know that you're OK. She knows you're out of danger. That's unless you resort to your old ways. Then I cannot help you," said Greg with a laugh.

"Thanks, I'm sure she wants to hear my voice. Bye," commented Reece.

Calling Tori Reece said, "Hi, honey. Sorry I'm calling so late."

"Oh, Reece, it's so good to hear your voice. I did hear from Greg that you were no longer in danger. But I didn't realize you really were in danger. Oh, what a fool I am. When are you coming home?"

"We leave tomorrow morning," replied Reece.

"I know it's only been one week, but it seems like forever. With the international flights being shut down, the funeral for the vice president and news blackout on what was really happening, it was stressful. I understand your passion for what you used to do, but I'm not made of the same stuff!" Tori carried on, now releasing her anxiety from the past week.

"I know. I'll stay clear of the government from now on. The project was fun and exciting, but the results were really overwhelming. This is exactly why I retired from all of that. Love you," Reece said.

"Bye, love you, too," said Tori as she hung up.

CHAPTER TEN

Sunday

Taipei Airport

The personnel from the US embassy escorted Henry, with his arm in a sling, and Reece and Sarah to the gate. They had been informed that this team had intercepted the assassin behind the vice president's death.

Greg did get them seats in Business Class. When they got on the plane, the purser greeted Henry as an old friend. It was Natalie Matins, the purser on the flight Henry took to Taipei. "Henry, it's so good to see you! Is this going to be a less exciting flight?" said Natalie with a smile and a wink.

"Are you ok?" she continued, noticing his arm in a sling.

"Yes, and only if you don't run out of red wine," replied Henry.

"Not a problem for you. I have to let the captain know you're aboard. It's Jim Watts. I heard there was a mucky-muck the US embassy was putting aboard. Are these your friends?" continued Natalie.

"Yes, we work together," answered Henry.

Sarah and Reece exchanged looks, both questioning how Henry had charmed this veteran flight attendant. They both smiled and went to their assigned seats.

The flight was long, but all three did manage to fall asleep, knowing they had accomplished the mission that was asked of them. Next stop: Home sweet home.

Schenectady, New York

Reece got into the Albany, New York, airport at 10:20 p.m. Waiting outside the security area was Tori. She was tearing up, and smiling ear to ear. She ran to Reece. They embraced for close to a minute before anything was said.

"I have missed you," Tori said. "I'm so relieved you're OK."

"Me too. It may have only been a week in calendar time but it seemed like much more," said Reece.

"What can you tell me?" asked Tori.

"Everything. There is nothing classified now. We have destroyed the two hearing devices that left the country," said Reece.

"To be precise, there is one still with Jeff in Washington and the one in my ear", thought Reece.

"Is the government going to be upset?" asked Tori.

"Perhaps, but we found out how dangerous the devices can be, especially in the wrong hands."

"What's going to happen to Jeff, Henry, and Greg?"

"They get to go back to what they were doing. Bruce Hardy will be happy to have them back. I have a lot of calls to make tomorrow after I wake up, to thank a whole lot of people for helping me," continued Reece.

"Next week we will get together with the Team in Washington and celebrate. Apparently Jeff is bummed out that he could not get the assassination of the VP out of his perpetrator. They apparently keep everything compartmentalized so no one knows everything. He will be there. We need to cheer him up," said Reece.

"I know about the celebration. Greg and I have developed a great relationship. I put in to take the time off."

"How is Professor Quinn?"

"He has physically recovered. He is home now, and Anne is doting on him. He loves it. It was a wakeup call for both of them. I heard they are going to go away on a long vacation," answered Tori. "What about the antidote you told me about?"

"That's to be our secret. As far as the government is concerned, it does not exist," answered Reece.

"You'd better not use it on me!" exclaimed Tori.

"Ha, that's good. I'm not sure the system can read your mind. There is a limit to technology," said Reece, knowing he was now getting into hot water and a place he did not want to be. He loved this woman more than anything and would never violate her trust in him.

As soon as Reece saw his checked bag on the carousel he grabbed it and said, "I'm going to sleep until noon tomorrow." Both headed to the airport exit.

As they got into the car, Tori turned to Reece and with a serious tone asked, "Is doing work for the country out of your system now?"

"Oh, yes. I quit once. This was an exception because I knew I was the only one who could complete this mission. I'm all yours," Reece said with conviction.

"Can I call my dad and tell him we'll be visiting next weekend?" asked Tori.

"If he'll let me come. You still want me?" answered Reece with a wink.

"I sure hope I can keep my promise to not come to the aid of my country again. It's a mistress like no other. My love for my country is as passionate as my love for Tori, just different."

<<<◇>>>

New Techno Thriller

Link to Amazon

Available in either paperback and ePub

HEAR YOU THINK

Alexander Gelson

web site link: www.alexandergelston.com